THE WIDOW AND THE ROGUE

Book 3
Gentlemen of Honor Series

by

Beverly Adam

Lachesis
Publishing Inc

www.lachesispublishing.com

Published Internationally by Lachesis Publishing Inc.
Rockland, Ontario, Canada

A catalogue record for the print format of this title
is available from the National Library of Canada

ISBN 978-1-927555-46-0

A catalogue record for the Ebook is available
from the National Library of Canada
Ebooks are available for purchase from
www.lachesispublishing.com

ISBN 978-1-927555-45-3

Editor: Joanna D'Angelo

Copyeditor: Giovanna Lagana

Dedication

For my parents, John and Diane, who always have a book in their hands. I hope you enjoy this one.

Acknowledgments

To the wonderful team at Lachesis Publishing. Thank you for your creative contributions to this book and to the entire Gentlemen of Honor trilogy. Your work made each story a better one. Bravo!

Also available

Gentlemen of Honor Series
The Spinster and the Earl (Book 1)
The Lady and the Captain (Book 2)

THE WIDOW AND THE ROGUE

Chapter 1

Lady Kathleen Langtry awoke with a gasp. The sound of a high-pitched scream had startled her out of a deep slumber. Bracing herself, she sat up, pulling back the heavy gold bed curtains. . . ."

Heart pounding, she slipped out of bed and opened wide the wood shutters. Peering out, she tried to locate the cause of that heartrending cry. A sudden gust of cold wind blew across the lake below, rippling its dark waters. This eastern red wind, the Irish said, was capable of blasting trees and skinning flesh off men. It was dangerous, believed to be magical and powerful.

She looked down the green slope to the water. She noticed a small cluster of white beech trees lit by the moon's pale light. Their leaves rustled noisily in the wind. Legend said the *daione sidhe,* the fairies, used the small arbor to create a magic ring of power. It helped them to conjure up enchantments—spells used to control and interfere in the lives of ordinary mortals.

Suddenly, a dense mist rose up from the water. A ghostly form began to take shape. It appeared to be a heavily veiled woman. The figure stood forlornly by the lapping water of the lake's rocky edge, and then began to wail in a chanting, plaintive moan, "Dead . . . dead . . . dead . . ." The unearthly specter quivered, its pale arms raised in a gesture of grief. In front of her astonished eyes the shrouded being glided forward, long strands of silver hair floating behind it. Its translucent limbs moved slowly, drifting up to the moon's bright light. In midair the spirit groaned. Its mouth opened wide to emit a soul-piercing wail. The cry escalated into a terrifying scream . . .

Kathleen shuddered, watching. She could feel her heart pounding with fear. Frightened, she hugged herself for comfort. If another person had been present, she would have undoubtedly clung to him.

The apparition's long robes billowed in the wind. The veil covering its face glowed eerily beneath. With one final moan of pronounced doom, it cried, "Dead . . . " one final time, then evaporated into the moonlight.

"A *ban-si.*" Kathleen breathed, recognizing the unearthly being. She rubbed her eyes, not quite believing what she had just seen.

A real banshee . . .

The female spirit was a well-known harbinger of death. The spirit held secrets only immortal beings possessed, her wail a foretelling of a person's imminent demise.

Kathleen, like everyone else, knew that the banshee's name was derived from the Irish Gaelic word, *van*, meaning "a woman of beauty." For the Irish reasoned death could be both horrific and beautiful as the frightening *ban-si* spirit, signifying both an end and a new beginning.

But why was she wailing? Was someone at the manor about to die or already dead? Goosebumps rose up along her arms in alarm. She didn't know, and it was a disquieting thought.

Chilled, she took a paisley shawl from a chair and draped it over her shoulders. She'd just been a witness to the announcement of someone's death. It was a dreadful foretelling. And there was nothing she could do to prevent it.

The Catholic monastery, Dovehill Hall, was built upon what had once been a sacred Druid burial ground. It had been taken over by the apostatizing Roman Catholic monks centuries ago. But Kathleen had never before seen evidence of the legend that connected the hill and lake to the powerful fey . . . until now.

*   *   *

Placing slippers upon her feet, she left the safety of her bedchamber, but she was not alone. A few of the servants were holding candles aloft in trembling hands. They wandered around the dark corridors seeking each other out. Frightened, they too had been awakened by the spirit's soul-piercing screams.

Oddly, the one person she had expected to see did not make an appearance. Where was Mrs. O'Grady, the domineering housekeeper? She should be there dourly glowering at everyone to remain calm. But she was not.

"Lady Langtry," said one of the young maids, hurrying up to her. "You are t' come quick, ma'am. There's been a terrible accident. And I was told to fetch ye. Please, come with me, my lady."

She nodded dumbly, not thinking to ask what had happened. But she could tell from the tremor in the girl's voice that something had. She wondered if it was connected with the banshee's wailing. This last thought sent her heart pounding with worried anticipation.

"Lead the way," she said and gathered her shawl more tightly around her.

The girl ran ahead through the crowd of servants standing in the corridor. A few had already begun weeping. Sensing the urgency of the situation, she started to run as well, pursuing the girl through a series of corridors and doors leading to the oldest part of the hall. She slowed as they entered the east wing. It connected to the ruined monastery and its nearby round stone tower.

The girl stopped, opening wide a heavy door. They crossed a flag-stoned terrace. On one side, it overlooked the ruins and on the other, the lake. Kathleen spotted a group of people clustered in a tight circle below. Some of the servants held candles or lanterns, casting a glow over a figure. A body lay on the ground. But who it was, she could not see.

"Be careful," the girl warned as they descended a narrow staircase.

She took heed. The steps leading down were well-worn and slippery. They were once part of the ruined monastery. There wasn't any protective railing to keep one from falling—only open air.

A brisk wind whipped through the nearby trees, scattering dead leaves in a swirling motion. She wore a thin chemise under her shawl. She shivered. It would be a wonder if she did not catch a chill—the night air was bitingly cold and damp.

She leaned into the thick wall, her hands touching the stone for support. She didn't wish to lose her balance. She glanced down. The ruins below housed a cemetery and a medieval chapel, both built in the Eleventh Century. The marble crosses and raised tombstones of dead monks glowed forebodingly in the moonlight. If she missed a step, she would quickly be joining them.

Carefully, she descended, step by step . . .

She breathed a small sigh of relief upon reaching the last one. Her feet rested again on solid ground.

"Here we are, ma'am," said the girl, leading her to the circle.

The servants drew back. She entered the enclosure. Immediately, she recognized the person lying in the center.

It was her husband, the elderly Lord Bangford Langtry.

* * *

The local surgeon approached. He put a comforting hand on her shoulder.

"I'm sorry . . . he's dead, Lady Langtry" he said, shaking his head. "He must have fallen backwards into the chapel. Heavens knows why a man in his fragile condition should decide to try and use those unsafe stairs. It is quite beyond my understanding."

He pointed to the staircase located on the other side of the terrace.

It was similar to the one she had used to come down. There was no protective railing. It led from the top of the high, round tower, one of the oldest buildings connected with the hall and ruins, to the monastery chapel below.

The *cloigtheach* tower, as it was known in Irish, soared three stories above the ground. It had a conical-shaped roof and was higher than the tallest tree in Urlingford. It was built to protect the monks from fierce Viking raiders.

Local legend said the tower held mystical qualities associated with the positioning of the moon and stars. It was much like the ones stargazers used for astrology, mapping out the future through constellations, but until tonight she had experienced no unearthly connections. This was the first time a powerful spirit had made its presence known. And it appeared in order to make a terrifying prediction. One connected with death.

Shattered glass lay around her dead husband's body. Bangford had lost his balance and fallen straight through the huge, stained-glass window of the chapel. He'd been impaled by thousands of shards—a sudden and gruesome ending to his life.

She walked into the sanctuary. Glass crunched beneath her slipper-clad feet. An angel's smile looked up at her from the chapel floor. Try as she might she could not conjure up any feelings of grief. She was in shock, overcome by jarred nerves and fright. An enveloping numbness possessed her.

Standing before the chapel's simple wooden cross, her thoughts dwelt upon the first time she'd met her husband.

Lord Bangford Langtry had been a collector of rare and beautiful objects. At the age of fifteen, she attracted the attentions of the wealthy connoisseur. Much as he did with his other valuable objects, his lordship obtained her through a third party, her greedy uncle, Squire Lynch.

For years the unfeeling spendthrift had been acting as her legal guardian. Little by little he recklessly squandered away her inheritance. When he sold off the last of her deceased parents' silver, any remaining shred of moral sensibility he possessed had vanished along with her inheritance.

Unfortunately, he discovered a new way to pay off his many debts. And this scheme involved her, his only living relative. He decided to sell her off to the highest bidder as a child bride, giving a feeble excuse.

"Because you've become too costly to clothe and feed, m-m'dear," he stuttered as his tailor placed the finely embroidered waistcoat around him. "I've decided to find you a husband. One who will be able to t-take care of you p-properly.

"But, Uncle, I am but fifteen," she reminded him. The minimum age for legal wedlock in Ireland was sixteen.

"And-a-half . . . I'm f-fair certain we can find some way around the issue of your tender age. Nay, there is no need to thank me," he said, waving a heavily bejeweled hand in the air. "I am only doing my duty as any good guardian would. On the m-morrow I have arranged for you to meet your prospective groom."

"But I—"

"It is settled, Kathleen. You are to be married to the man I have chosen for you. I am your legal guardian. I know what is best for you."

Refusing to hear another word, he strode off to meet his solicitor. There in the legal chambers, he signed the binding marriage contract, coldly inking in her name.

Lord Bangford Langtry was the parish's elderly magistrate. With nary a look of regret on his pasty face, Uncle Lynch introduced her to the decrepit old man.

"My good sir, may I present to you my ward and niece, Lady Kathleen Dargheen," he said, giving a low bow. The braces supporting his artificial muscles audibly squeaked beneath his yellow silk coat.

She remembered her uncle practicing for hours in front of the mirror, the perfect serpentine *S* for the bow. She stood beside him at the entrance to the hall's oriental salon in her simple, gray walking gown.

She curtsied to the old gentleman, eyeing him warily. Surely he must be my prospective groom's grandfather, she told herself reassuringly, not imagining for a moment that her uncle expected her to wed this relic of decaying manhood.

She'd thought long and hard about her fate, and reluctantly she'd accepted it. She had no choice. Running away was not an option.

Orphaned, alone, and friendless, she was entirely at the mercy of these two men. She had no monetary resources, proper education, or ability to do anything but what was expected of her. She had no choice. The law, she knew, would not help her. Legally, she was under her uncle's care, and therefore his thumb. And now she was about to become his unwilling sacrifice.

No words were spoken. Lord Langtry, seated in an ornately carved walnut bishop's chair, waved them into the silk-tented room. The chair upon which he sat had once belonged to a Roman Catholic bishop.

The original monastery had been ransacked and burned to the ground by Oliver Cromwell in 1641, during the notorious massacres. The chair, along with the monastery and the lands surrounding it, had passed into Protestant hands and eventually into the wealthy English lord's.

He had the monastery transformed into Dovehill Hall, a Regency Gothic mansion situated on a high knoll, overlooking a bucolic lake. The hall was designed by an Italian architect who'd attempted to emulate James Wyatt's and Robert Smirke's graceful and refined medieval styles. But instead of a whimsical Gothic structure, a glum, square building arose, a four-towered monstrosity unsuccessfully incorporating the old with the new.

The old lord removed a gold monocle from his smoking jacket. Squinting through it, he looked her over from head to toe.

"Take off your bonnet," he commanded.

She released the faded blue ribbons with trembling fingers. Careful, so as not to disarrange her hair, she removed it. Her uncle had warned her beforehand that the old lord was particular about appearances.

The gold-colored strands shone under the room's candlelight. Her hair was considered to be one of her most remarkable features. There were not many women who had the unusual color. In the past it had been much commented upon, along with her large china-blue eyes.

She, however, felt wretched.

She was ill at ease standing there in front of the old man as he minutely inspected her. She did not have the comfort of being well-gowned for this important meeting. The walking frock she wore was outdated and fitted poorly.

Inwardly, she sighed, thinking about all the beautiful clothes she had once owned. They'd been sold off long ago to pay for her uncle's many gambling debts.

The faded attire was an embarrassment. Her ankles showed immodestly below the hem. And adding to her

[18]

unease was the tight bodice. Her young bosom filled it
to almost bursting . . . it was discomforting.

She stood in this imposing building, the home of her
future groom, dressed in castoff clothes like a lowly
scullery maid. *What must his grandfather think of me?*
She wondered miserably as his watery eyes observed
her.

She pulled her shawl tightly over her exposed bosom.

He must surely think me the most immodest of
women, not fit to marry his grandson . . . and I would
not blame him if he refused to accept me.

But the old lord said nothing about her attire as he
carefully looked her over.

His balding head was covered by a round Turkish
cap with a dangling gold tassel. He held in one hand a
long polished walking cane with the head of a roaring
lion carved in gold. He looked as if he were leaning
forward. This, she noted, was due to his humped back. A
deformity brought about by the ravages of old age.

"She is as you described her, Squire," he said at last,
nodding.

The gold tassel on his cap swung back and forth like
a pendulum. "She is quite splendid to look at, young,
delicate of bone, with dainty ankles, a fine bosom, and a
trim figure to match. Aye, she may very well do as my
future bride. Many men, including those much younger
than I, would envy me."

Upon hearing the old lord's pronouncements
concerning herself as his future wife, she suddenly felt
lightheaded. A roiling, sick feeling entered the pit of her
stomach.

Three servants standing discretely in a corner of the
room noted her reaction.

The oldest servant, a woman with graying hair,
wearing a black-striped house dress, openly glowered at
her. Her slanted eyes sparkled dangerously. It was as if

Beverly Adam

she was silently daring Kathleen to faint. The other two, a teenaged serving girl and a footman, looked over at the young beauty with unspoken compassion.

The salon was cluttered with ivory miniatures, marble-white pedestal tables, sandalwood pagodas, painted white elephants, as well as silk wall coverings. But she cared not a wit for any of these exotic ornaments. It felt as if she was standing on the edge of a damning abyss instead of in a silk-covered salon.

She took a horrified step back.

One thought repeated itself in her mind . . . *my uncle expects me to marry this dreadful old man . . . my uncle expects me to marry . . .*

Stunned by the terrible realization she was being given to this leering, old codger, her face turned ashen.

Lord Langtry made a bored circling gesture with his cane. It reminded her of the local auction hawker. When he was selling off horses, he prodded the animals into a galloping motion using a sharp stick. She was being treated in the same uncaring manner.

"Turn around, my dear, so Lord Langtry may see the back of you," her uncle said, interpreting the gesture.

"Oh my . . . yes . . . yes, indeed . . ." The old man sighed, with the click clacking of his false front teeth, as if indeed she was a dumb animal and had no feelings.

Slowly, trembling with fear and loathing, she turned.

Lord Langtry never took his eyes off her. Smiling, he tapped her with his cane's lion head.

"She's quite untouched you say . . . Never been kissed, girl?" he asked, his few remaining teeth contrasting with the porcelain ones.

Silently, she shook her head no.

Not caring about his niece's obvious distress, her uncle agreed. He rubbed his hands together with glee. He happily noticed the wealthy lord's interest.

"See the fleece I wear about my neck, child? It's

[20]

quite soft to the touch . . . come here and I will let you feel it," Lord Langtry said.

Fearful, hating the way he ogled her, she took another step back. But her uncle pushed her towards him.

"Touch it," commanded the old man, fingering the skin.

She leaned over. With the tips of her fingers, she did as she was told. The lambskin was soft and wiry. She didn't know why, but the thought of the dead animal brought tears to her eyes.

Lord Langtry roughly pulled her onto his lap.

She squirmed, trying to remove his hand. But surprisingly, he held her firmly in place. His arms were strong. He brought his hand around her, using his gold cane as a barrier, blocking her attempt to escape.

His left hand, the color of faded parchment, picked up a handful of her gold hair. He let the strands fall gently through his trembling fingers. He reached out and touched the smooth pink of her unblemished cheek.

"Release me, sir." She breathed, continuing her struggle. He would not budge. He smiled blissfully at her distress.

Exasperated, angry at being held against her will, she gave him a sharp kick in the shins. The manservant standing in the corner snickered.

"My dear Kathleen, you really should not have done that," her uncle protested weakly, afraid the bags of coins he had seen earlier would now disappear.

Lord Langtry, with a grimacing wince of pain, opened his arms.

She quickly jumped off his lap and walked to the ornate French doors. But her way was blocked. The old woman dressed in the black-striped gown stood in front of them. She later learned the old bat was Mrs. O'Grady, the housekeeper.

She glared angrily at Kathleen.

"You kicked Lord Langtry," the woman muttered, "and embarrassed him in front of the servants. That's unforgivable. You ought to be punished."

She could have sworn the snarling woman blocking her way would have taken great pleasure at that moment, if she could, at pulling out every hair on her head. She had balled her hands into defensive fists.

She decided if the older woman dared to touch her, she would give her a facer. One the interfering hag would not soon forget.

Lord Langtry interceded, slowly inclining his head. The housekeeper obediently stepped aside. Kathleen walked with determined dignity through the doors into the hall's foyer. There she broke into a run, making her short-lived escape.

The last words she heard were, "So how much do you want for the chit?" And she knew her fate was sealed. One week later, special license in hand, a bribed priest in tow, she was hastily married off to the old lord she had been forced to call "husband" these past three years.

* * *

Looking down at the body of the man she had once been forcibly wed to, she didn't feel anything. She was numb. If he had been kind to her, and caring, she could have been content, no matter his age, after having spent her young life at the mercy of her selfish uncle . . . but her husband had never been kind, or caring . . . and now he was gone. She was no longer his plaything, an object he owned, and wanted other men to envy and admire. She was no longer to be ordered about.

He was dead.

Bangford will never be able to touch me again, she thought, hugging herself.

Perhaps it was instinct or simply the need to be nearer to the one who held power over life and death that propelled her to walk up to the front of the chapel, but when she reached the altar, she noticed an object lying upon it.

She picked it up.

It appeared to be an antique brooch from the medieval period. Made of gold and copper, it was studded with glass and covered in Celtic motifs. In particular, she noted the intricate design.

Stamped in gold, twining itself around the clasp, the unbroken Celtic interlacing, known as the lovers' knot, ornamented the pin. She knew it was symbolic of the connection each person shared with others in both life and death. The knot was representative of the eternal nature of love. It went on and on . . . never ending.

Some of the servants, upon seeing what she held, quickly crossed themselves. They looked at each other apprehensively. The piece of jewelry might contain black magic.

A few whispered, "The banshee left it there for her to find . . . it's a gift from the dead."

No one asked to examine it.

The servants believed the object to be from the underworld. They feared it might be enchanted or cursed. Another evil omen foretelling a future demise, they believed, was woven within its elaborate golden design. It was best, they told each other, to stay away from such dark magic. It could kill you.

Kathleen, fascinated by the unusual ornament, pinned it onto her shawl.

For a reason she could not explain, she too felt it was a sign. Her life had been forever changed. She was at last free of the odious man who had possessed her, but had never loved or respected her.

Perhaps, she told herself, *I will at last be free and find the happiness that has eluded me since I was a child living with my parents, and finally live the way I want.*

She envisioned herself for a moment as an old woman surrounded by her children and grandchildren. She would have her portrait painted wearing the brooch as she held her youngest grandchild on her lap—his tiny, chubby hand would reach up to touch the enchanting ornament.

She sensed, as she imagined this family scene, that one day she would at last find what she had been missing to make her life a happy one . . . love. From that moment onwards, she never took off the brooch. It became her talisman of hope.

Chapter 2

The funeral was a quiet affair. The mourners comprised of the servants of the hall, a few of the villagers, her uncle, and some of the local aristocrats, including her late husband's sister, the Countess Henrietta Deuville and her corpulent son, Henry. The latter had the family trait of watery gray eyes. Of course, Mrs. O'Grady, the housekeeper, was there as well, frowning as usual.

But there was one gentleman who had made an unexpected appearance. The sight of this handsome dandy standing at her late husband's gravesite caused her to take a quick breath of surprise.

"Beau Powers," she whispered to herself, upon sighting the profile of the noted Corinthian.

She'd heard he was now a renowned solicitor. He'd gained a reputation after handling several high profile cases for the Golden Clover elite, the titled and wealthy of Irish society, many of whom the solicitor counted as friends. Over the years, she'd also heard the maids and local townspeople gossip about his mistresses, including a famous ballerina from Russia and an actress from London. Yes, he was known, almost as much for his romantic affairs as he was for his legal ones.

It had been a little over a year since she had last seen him. She'd been seventeen at the time, an unworldly young woman confined to living a restricted life in the village of Urlingford. The sight of such a handsome, self-assured gentleman up close, she remembered, had been like seeing a shooting star for the first time, completely unexpected and thrilling.

She quickly noted that he'd remained the same manly nonpareil she'd first observed him to be. The arrogant tilt of his head was unmistakable. His thick, guinea-colored hair, however, was not coiffed in the fashionable style inspired by the legendary Lord Wellington, the hero of the decisive battle of Waterloo. Instead, he wore it in a simpler manner, one that would not require hours of styling.

He was still the muscular, well-kept gentleman she first met when she disguised herself as a page boy to deliver news of the whereabouts of the then kidnapped Lady Beatrice O'Brien. She remembered the first time she had laid eyes on him. He was standing beside his friend, the handsome Earl of Drennan, who'd launched the search for his beloved Lady Beatrice, after she'd been kidnapped by the evil Viscount Linley, her former fiancé. That loathsome toad had kidnapped the wealthy heiress, known as the Spinster of Brightwood Manor, to force her hand in marriage. The earl, who'd fallen in love with Lady Beatrice, had gone after them, his good friend Beau Powers by his side. The Earl of Drennan was indeed handsome with his rugged good looks, but Beau Powers was simply beautiful, like a statue of a Greek god.

She'd never before seen such a man. Compared to her odious, shriveled husband, he was the epitome of youthful manhood. When his striking blue eyes had smiled at her, she'd felt a lightning bolt of awareness course through her body, making her toes curl. She'd been completely awestruck.

The Earl of Drennan had noticed her reaction and said, "Looks as if you've snared yourself another admirer, Beau."

Her face had flushed at the comment. But she had been truly mortified when Beau had stared at her, for she was wearing rags, hiding her true gender and station in life.

She'd cleverly disguised herself as a stable boy in order to escape the watchful eyes of Mrs. O'Grady, the housekeeper, who was the intimidating woman her husband had appointed to guard her. She'd been essentially kept a prisoner in her own home, unable to do what she'd wanted for her entire marriage.

But upon learning of the kidnapped Lady Beatrice's secret whereabouts during a dinner party hosted by her husband, she'd vowed to help her escape. She'd not wanted the dear lady to share her fate and be trapped in a similar marriage to a coldhearted, domineering man.

She'd heard that Beau Powers had been the first to volunteer to help the Earl of Drennan. They said he'd stood by his friend throughout the daring rescue, risking his own life against a room full of cutthroat mercenaries, who'd been hired by Linley. During the ensuing brawl, it was he who enabled the earl to defeat the viscount by throwing him a sword just in time as the viscount charged the earl with a blade of his own.

* * *

Aye, Beau had not changed a wit, she decided glancing at him. Outwardly, he'd remained the epitome of gentlemanly perfection. She could tell by the way his double-breasted coat stretched across his broad shoulders and the authentic manner in which his breeches fit around his trim waist that he carried none of the usual corpulent fat associated with other gentlemen of the ton. That was not surprising, considering he was both a noted horseman, as well as an excellent marksman.

But did he always behave in such an honorable manner? She frowned, doubting. She was reminded of the expression that stated clothes did not make the man. He hadn't become a top solicitor in court by being nice. Such men were known to be heartless rogues of the first order. She'd merely to remember how the law had overlooked her being underage when she was forced to marry at fifteen to Lord Langtry, to know rules were easily broken by such men.

And she knew he could be at times ruthless—even in her small country village, rumors of his exploits were repeated by the gossipmongers. They discussed with avid interest, the duels he fought when challenged by those who lost their cases to him in court. In anger, the losers chose to settle the matter again with drawn swords, fruitlessly hoping to achieve a more favorable end. But that never happened. Master Powers had always been the victor. And any man with a bit of common sense would not dare to challenge such a skilled fighter, unless he had a secret death wish.

She shuddered, thinking of his piercing eyes when she'd spoken to him and the earl about the kidnappers. His had been filled with deadly intent. Faith, she would not want to be the man facing him at the sharp end of a sword.

But what was he doing here? She wondered, peeking up at him through her heavy widow's veil. His solicitor's business was located in Tipperary—why was he attending her husband's funeral? To her knowledge her late husband and the handsome Corinthian were not known to one another.

Could it be he was here because of her? Her heart pounded a little at the audacious thought. But she quickly dismissed it as an improbability.

For who was she to him? No one.

She hadn't seen him since the kidnapping of Lady Beatrice. It was the only time they'd ever met. And she knew he'd not known who she was back then.

She glanced back to take a better look at him. What purpose had brought him to Dovehill Hall? Did it involve her husband's death? Or was he here for some other reason?

Unbeknownst to Kathleen, he was there for all

three—she was soon to discover the reason why. And it very much involved her.

*   *   *

When the short service ended, Kathleen's uncle led her back to the hall. He was acting very solicitous of her, which she expected given the size of her husband's estate, and her uncle's greedy nature. A hearty repast had been laid out for the wake, but she didn't partake. She had no appetite. Her stomach was in knots, so she merely fidgeted with the plate of food a servant handed her. It was time for the reading of her husband's will. She was finally to learn her fate.

Either she was to continue the controlled life she had been leading until now, dominated by the housekeeper and her in-laws—or perhaps, and this next thought caused her a surge of hope—her late husband's relatives would inherit Dovehill Hall and she would at last be set free to live an unencumbered life.

That was indeed wishful thinking. She sighed.

She'd noticed the leering manner in which her nephew, Henry, inspected her. His watery eyes deliberately stared at her well-covered bosom. It was as if he were mentally undressing her—waiting for the moment until he could lay his pudgy hands upon her.

Feeling a wave of sickness overcome her, she handed the untouched plate to a passing servant. The idea of Henry touching her was repulsive—a continuation of the nightmare she'd been living. From past experience, she recalled how Henry had treated her . . . like a woman of easy virtue. Despite being his uncle's wife, Henry would reach out and touch her in an unwelcome manner whenever she passed him in the dimly lit corridors of Dovehill Hall. In the dark she would gasp in shocked surprise at his audacity. He would laugh, enjoying her obvious discomfort.

She had mentioned these humiliating moments to her husband. But he'd paid no heed. He'd dismissed the episodes as nothing more than boyish pranks. He told her she had an overactive imagination and had mistaken Henry's intentions.

"He's just having a bit of high-spirited fun. Do try to be less of a country innocent," he'd say and that would be the end of it.

Grimly, she decided she would run away and become a nun before she would permit Henry or any other man to ever again rule her life. But she set aside those glum thoughts, deciding to patiently await the reading of the will. It was her only hope.

*   *   *

As the mantle clock bonged the hour, the family met in the red salon. To her surprise, Beau Powers stood by the marble fireplace waiting for them to enter.

"Lady Langtry," he said approaching her, his brilliant, sapphire eyes never leaving hers. "May I tell you how truly sorry I am for your loss. Such a regrettable accident . . . how terrible it must have been for you."

"Thank you, sir," she replied, barely able to speak as he took her hand.

He bowed over it.

"It is most gracious of you to be concerned, Master Powers. But why are you—"

"Why am I here?" he said, finishing the sentence for her. "Indeed, you must be astonished to see me. Especially considering the unique circumstances under which we last had the pleasure to meet."

He smiled down at her. A faint dimple appeared at the corner of his lips.

She couldn't help but return it, despite the somber event taking place. She remembered the moment when one year ago her broad, brim hat had flown off. Her golden hair had tumbled down to reveal that she was not a serving boy, but a young woman in disguise. She'd laughed at his stunned expression and merrily rode off on her pony, having accomplished her mission of informing the rescuers as to the kidnapped Lady Beatrice's whereabouts, which she'd overheard being discussed when her husband invited Viscount Linley and a priest to dine with them.

Aye, she smiled. He remembered that moment, too. It had been one of the few happy ones she'd had during the last few years. The restraints of where she was allowed to go, and with whom she was allowed to associate, had been very limiting.

She'd never been permitted to go anywhere, unless she was accompanied by her husband or the housekeeper. With the exception of the bilious toadies her husband invited to dinner, she saw no one and had not a single friend she could count upon.

"I am to act in the place of your husband's solicitor," he explained. "The one he had originally hired preceded him in death. It occurred two days in advance of this dreadful accident. I suppose your husband had not yet been notified before he died?"

She shook her head. And if Bangford had been informed of the death, she knew he would not have confided in her. He'd kept her ignorant concerning all his legal affairs. All of this was a revelation.

He continued, "And so it is that I am here. My reputation, it would appear, has spread further than Tipperary County. Until a senior solicitor can be found to replace me, I have been asked to take over the practice and help the partnership in Dublin."

"Indeed . . . how interesting," she replied, surprised by the unusual circumstances that had brought them together once more.

"Yes," he smiled down at her, "it appears to be our destiny to meet again . . . but now I must perform the duty that has been placed in my hands."

Purposefully, he picked up a document from the mantle. He looked about the room at the assembled family, the glum housekeeper, and the elderly members of the staff who had served Dovehill Hall for years.

"Ah, I see everyone is present. You may close the doors," he informed an elderly footman standing nearby.

"Now, dear lady, if you will but seat yourself," he said leading her solicitously to a chair. "I shall begin to read your late husband's will."

She sat quietly and listened as he read the document aloud. Her husband had left the usual legacies to the elderly servants of long service, including pensions and promised tenant cottages. The legacies were within the norm, with the exception of Mrs. O'Grady's, who was deeded an entire house and land.

The remainder of the legacies for the servants of long service occasioned no comments. Pleased faces and nods were given as the staff recognized their names and were told what they had been bequeathed.

When he had finished with this portion, Beau turned the paper over and said pointedly, "Those in service may retire. I shall begin reading the part of the will that concerns only the immediate family."

After the servants had left, the housekeeper still stood by the door. Her formidable presence was tangibly felt. She sullenly crossed her arms and scowled. She waited for him to continue reading.

He noticed and remarked calmly, "You may go as well, Mrs. O'Grady. Your presence is no longer required."

"But as head of the servants in service here, I have a right to know what is to happen to the hall," she said with a small sniff.

She looked pointedly over at Kathleen and Lord Langtry's relatives.

"I ought to be told who will be the next master or mistress here. So I may inform the others as to who we will owe our living."

This comment included Squire Lynch, Lord Langtry's sister, the Countess Deuville, and Henry. The countess, who until now wore a bored expression, transformed into someone keenly interested as to what was about to take place. This was also true of Henry, who had been quietly snoring in a corner. His hands clasped over his protruding middle.

They may rightly assume Lord Langtry has put them in charge over me and Dovehill Hall, decided Kathleen, inwardly sighing.

She did not trust any of them. They were all cut from the same cloth. As an underage widow not yet one and twenty, she knew one of them might be named her legal guardian. Her life, it would appear, was fated never to be her own.

Looking at the greed-filled faces, she could not decide who would make the better protector. To her knowledge they were all equally dreadful. And from past experiences, she knew they would enjoy controlling her.

Another thought entered her mind . . . Henry might be given the entire estate as the sole surviving male relation. She would then be banished to the dowager house to live out the remainder of her days in genteel poverty.

She felt almost gleeful . . . the possibility of being left completely alone, without someone spying on her, caused a tiny smile to appear on her lips.

Privacy and freedom . . . two liberties she had been deprived of, would be hers. To regain them now would indeed create a blissful existence.

"Very well, Mrs. O'Grady," Beau said, conceding to the housekeeper's wish, "as it is in the interest of the new master of Dovehill Hall that the servants keep it running smoothly, you may stay and observe the proceedings."

He picked up the document again. "Ah yes," he said slowly, looking the testament over.

He did not look up. He gave no indication as to who would be put in charge of her and Dovehill Hall. She sensed, however, that he knew.

Master Powers had undoubtedly read over the will several times. He was, she could tell by his severe professional manner, putting on a show. It was to give extra weight to the papers he held.

None of them, she knew, would be able to dispute the validity of Bangford's will. It had been drawn up by one of the most noted law firms in Ireland. There would be no loopholes. It was unquestionably perfect.

He looked up and said with firm authority, "Here we are . . . hmm . . . let me sum up what it says . . . according to the last will and testament of Lord Bangford Langtry, it is his wife, Lady Kathleen, who will be mistress of Dovehill Hall."

Gasps of surprise went round the room.

He went on to explain, "Apparently, his lordship believed he was about to sire an heir, and therefore he decided to leave the entire estate in her ladyship's capable hands."

"That's preposterous!" the countess loudly protested from her chair.

Her white powdered face frowned with indignant disbelief. "She is but a child and quite clearly underage. As for offspring . . . my brother was too old to possibly beget any. This is entirely unthinkable!"

Noticing the housekeeper standing by the door, she added angrily, "To think I counted on you, O'Grady, to keep him from making such a terrible mistake! I told you to find him a nice elderly widow to marry. But instead he found this . . . this golden haired sorceress to tempt him."

The housekeeper did not defend herself. Instead the woman turned to Kathleen and with narrowed eyes said glumly, "I will turn my resignation in on the morrow, ma'am." She then faced the countess and added, "I thought he wanted to simply copulate with the bit—"

"Mrs. O'Grady," Beau broke in forcefully, not permitting her to continue. He firmly took the dour woman by the elbow and led her to the door.

"A grand shame you won't be staying on and all that . . . the house Lord Langtry deeded you is more than adequate compensation for your years of service. No need to worry about your notice. I am quite certain Lady Langtry will somehow manage without you. There appears to be at least a half dozen or more capable staff members who can take your place."

Looking down, he espied the heavy set of household keys hanging from the frowning woman's belt. They were the symbol of power she wielded over the entire hall and Kathleen.

"Oh, and by the by, it's very good of you to have the keys on hand. It will save her ladyship the effort of having to ask you to fetch them. Here, let me relieve you of the burden, since you will no longer have any use for them. I'll take them from you now, shall I?"

Before the housekeeper could protest, he unhooked the heavy chain from the glowering woman's waist. Keys clanked together as he held the large ring aloft.

"Why, I never in my entire life," muttered the offended lady, infuriated at his interference. "How dare you."

She tried to take them back.

He wagged a finger in front of her.

"But I do dare. And I am certain you never thought the day would come when the meek would inherit a bit of the earth," he said, firmly pushing her through the door. "Don't worry. I will make certain to have your position filled within the hour. There is no need for you to trouble yourself and stay on a minute longer, Mrs. O'Grady. Again, I am quite certain her ladyship will do perfectly well without you."

Mouth agape at his effrontery, the housekeeper watched him firmly shut the door in her face. He walked over and gently laid the keys in Kathleen's hands.

"They're yours to do with as you will, Lady Langtry," he said. "You are mistress here at Dovehill Hall." He added meaningfully to the others present, "No one else."

"Thank you, Master Powers," she said and felt a large lump develop in the back of her throat. Not since her parents' deaths had anyone defended her. This was the first time. She would never forget it.

"The pleasure, dear lady, is all mine," he said, bowing. "Now back to the business at hand."

He looked about the room at the remaining occupants. They all sat glumly observing him. They acted as if a prized golden egg had been stolen away by a conniving fox, not a dead man.

"Lord Langtry did not forget you," he said and lifting the will again, he began to read. "To my sister, the Countess Henrietta Deuville and my nephew, Henry, I leave an annuity of two thousand pounds each."

He looked at the document more closely.

"Lord Langtry has also bequeathed some rather unusual oddities. Including a rather naughty book of Indian block prints for you, Henry, and an exotic plant has been left for you, Countess. An insectivorous, a rare, fly-eating plant, I believe. Apparently, you had admired it once. Well, um, wasn't that thoughtful of his lordship?"

He beamed a grin at the white-powdered face before him.

The countess in turn glared at him.

Kathleen could not help but smile. Beau was clearly enjoying the moment. The sparkle of amusement in his clear blue eyes told her he was not taking any pains to hide that fact.

She understood why the countess was upset. A few thousand pounds and some queer oddities were nothing compared to what Dovehill Hall's estates generated annually. There was also the mysterious source of gems and valuable antiques that magically appeared from time to time to be auctioned off. They had paid for her late husband's costly imported eccentricities of exotic plants and rare oriental oddities.

But now Dovehill Hall's wealth would remain in her hands or that of her children, that is if she should decide to remarry. And as she was quite young, it was not an unrealistic expectation. Aye, her dead husband's family had good reason to be upset.

"Ahem." Her uncle, Squire Lynch, coughed delicately. "Did his lordship bequeath anything to me? I did after all introduce Kathleen to him. Surely that m-merited some sort of remembrance?"

Beau's eyebrows rose.

He peered down at the parchment before him, fingering it, line after line, to the very bottom. He stopped and gave the squire an affirmative nod. Lord Langtry apparently had not forgotten him.

The squire smiled back, a yellow-toothed, lopsided grin.

His choleric pale face was full of expectancy. A gleam brightened his droopy brown eyes. It was a familiar, greedy look that she recalled from the day he had given her to Lord Langtry. It made her insides queasy. This Judas would sell his own soul for a few pieces of gold.

Putting a hand into his right breast pocket, Beau withdrew a coin.

"Here," he said, putting it into Lynch's outstretched palm. "One farthing"

He read from the paper before him, speaking aloud the dead man's words. "To Squire Lynch, who gave me his niece for twenty-five bags of gold and then one month later asked for more . . . one farthing . . . the rascal doesn't merit two."

He stopped his reading and regarded the downcast face of the jackanapes before him. Lynch had obviously been hoping for substantially more.

"And on a personal note, Squire," he said, "I quite agree with his lordship. You are getting more than you deserve. I must say, a gentleman that sells his fifteen-year-old niece and only living relation to an old man almost five times her age deserves nothing but derision and sneering contempt."

The squire, dumbfounded, stared at the coin in his hand. He was stunned. He had just been given the cut direct from a dead man lying in his grave.

"Oh, and since we are talking about bad taste," Beau continued, his sharp blue eyes appraising the macaroon. "That puce colored waistcoat you are wearing is quite ghastly. Whoever your tailor is, he must be lacking in the upper stories to put that fabric on a choleric scarecrow such as yourself. To be blunt, sir, in my books you are nothing but a badly dressed cad."

He chose that moment to give Kathleen an unexpected wink.

She stared at him, hardly daring to believe what she had just seen and heard. The solicitor had put her uncle in his place. It was an unexpected victory. He was clearly taking her side.

Stunned, she looked towards her uncle, wondering what his reaction would be. Would he take offense? Would he rise up and give the cheeky solicitor a good facer?

But her uncle did nothing. He did not budge.

Nodding again, Lynch silently sank deeper into his chair. There was nothing he could do. The will was impenetrable. He would have to face the debt collectors empty-handed.

There was a reason why being in "dun territory" could have been easily known as being in "dung territory", for her uncle was once again deep in it. All the gold he'd been given by her late husband had been spent long ago.

"That is all," Beau said, straightening the sheath of papers in his hands. "Except for one minor bit of business that I must discuss with Lady Langtry in private, the reading of the last will and testament of Lord Bangford Langtry is concluded. If you have any questions, you may contact me at my Dublin chambers. I therefore bid you ladies and um, gentlemen, a pleasant good-day."

Thus dismissing them, he walked out of the room.

* * *

"Your husband, with good reason, trusted none of his relations to take care of your ladyship," Beau said, sipping a cup of jasmine tea as they sat in a small parlor on a brocade sofa. They now partook in a late afternoon repast of tea, sandwiches, pastries, and scones.

Her stomach audibly growled. He'd observed that she hadn't eaten all day. He glanced at her lovely face, red and embarrassed that he'd heard her growling stomach. He hid a smile. Poor woman, she had gone through a lot over the past few years. Beau stood up, and taking a plate of sandwiches, quietly offered them.

"I see that your ladyship was too occupied during your husband's wake to eat anything. May this help revive you," he said gently and handed it to her.

Unable to look him in the eye, she nodded and

whispered her thanks. She turned and took a few bites before asking optimistically, "Then no one is to have charge over me?"

He could see the glimmer of hope in her eyes and was glad that he was in a position to assist her. She seemed so demure, but he knew she had spirit. He'd seen it before—that day when she'd disguised herself as a lad to help them rescue Lady Beatrice.

"Not quite," he answered, looking directly at her. As he did so he was taken aback by her porcelain beauty— her pale skin, large blue eyes, and gold hair made her resemble one of the china dolls his sister used to own— delicate and fine.

She sat primly before him now, on her red velvet chair, a composed young woman dressed in black crepe. She appeared to be strong. But he feared something inside of her might snap and she would fall apart. He had a strong urge to protect her.

He remembered how he'd wanted to wrap his arms around her at the funeral but protocol had made it impossible. He was there representing her dead husband and the law. It would have been scandalous.

She'd looked so fragile and forlorn, standing alone by the graveside. No friends had stood by her. And he'd not seen her shed a single tear during the funeral. Her demeanor had been placid. It was as if she'd cut herself off from all emotion.

What had her life been like with old Lord Langtry and that domineering housekeeper? Had it been so terrible that she felt absolutely no grief for her husband? But then Lord Langtry had been an old man and an invalid. His death may have been anticipated. She may have already emotionally prepared for it. Still, he'd wondered at her relationship with her late husband. Had she grown to care for the old man? Had he treated her well? He wanted to know. For some reason it was important to him to know everything about her.

The corners of his eyes wrinkled a little in thought. She was far too young to be dressed in widow's weeds. With such lovely features, she would be desired by many men. They would want to attach themselves to her. She had both beauty and wealth to entice them. He pictured her being surrounded by ne'er-do-well vultures like her greedy uncle, men who would consider the young widow easy prey.

He frowned at the thought of the suave jackanapes she would soon encounter in Dublin ballrooms and salons—the type of gentlemen who thought nothing of charming a young widow into bed, merely for sport. Unconsciously, his fists tightened at his sides at the mere idea of her coming up against such deceiving charmers. He wanted to protect her against such cunning snakes.

"Are you well, Master Powers?" she asked, lifting an inquiring eyebrow at his clenched fists.

"Indigestion, I'm afraid," he lied with a tight smile. "Custard and I do not always get along. It's nothing to trouble your ladyship over."

Her mouth tightened a little, as though she was trying to hold back a smile at his comment. Well, at least she'd retained her sense of humor. But he silently berated himself for letting her see his inner turmoil concerning her well-being. He had to act in an impartial manner. He had to behave as if she were merely another client, not someone he would willingly fight off scheming rakes and fortune hunters for.

There was an untamed passion beneath her calm exterior. He'd glimpsed it a year ago when she'd aided Lady Beatrice. Defying her dominating husband, she'd disguised herself and helped the lady escape a forced marriage.

Despite having been controlled by others for most of

her young life, she still had a spark in her eyes, a bright light that said she was strong-willed and could be a handful. Aye, watching over her would be quite a lively undertaking.

"It appears that I'm to have the honor of acting as your guardian. If you desire, I will act in that capacity for a time," he said in a casual manner, testing her reaction to the news.

She turned two astonished eyes upon him.

"You?" she asked.

He bowed his head in acknowledgment. "Your husband had entrusted my predecessor to watch over you. Now, acting in the place of your husband's deceased solicitor, you and your estates have been placed entirely in my care."

She frowned. She couldn't help herself, but she did mind. She wanted her freedom, not another man ruling her life.

He noticed the flash of discontent in her eyes, but he could not find fault with it. If it had been him, he would have reacted in the same manner. For who would want another to rule over his life? No one, unless one was feeble-willed.

"There is no getting around it, your ladyship. You are under age and Irish law clearly states that someone older must act as your guardian until either you remarry or come of age. In this case, the guardian chosen by your husband's will is me."

"Are you to have absolute control over my life?" she asked with an edge in her voice. "Am I to have no say in the matter?"

"I have no dishonorable intentions towards you or any desire to impose my will over your own, Lady Langtry," he said reassuringly, reading her thoughts. "What I said earlier stands. You are mistress of Dovehill Hall. I am here to merely act as your mentor and advisor."

"I . . . I don't know what to say," she replied truthfully.

She gave him a mistrusting glance. Could he be counted upon? Was he speaking the truth? Or was he simply trying to placate her?

He leaned over and took her hand. She felt a sudden dryness in her mouth at his touch, his warmth disturbing.

At first he'd merely meant to reassure her, but now he couldn't help but notice how white and soft her skin felt beneath his, and how her touch heated his blood. He added pressure to his hold and they both felt a tingle of awareness course between them.

Startled, her eyes widened. She looked at him expectantly.

He took a deep breath and cleared his throat in order to continue. He had to find a way to explain himself. But at the same time he couldn't bring himself to release her hand from his. It was so soft.

"I shall behave like an older brother concerned only with protecting your interests," he said, although he felt far from brotherly feelings for her.

She bowed her head.

The feel of his hand over hers was enticing and invoked tender thoughts in her she'd thought long ago dead and buried with her parents. Doubt flooded her. She'd once trusted men. But she was now older and more cautious. She'd been badly hurt and callously used by them.

Would he betray her like her uncle had? Take all her money? Barter away her virtue? Or possibly use her, as Lord Langtry had, as some sort of rare possession to be shown off to the envy of other men?

She looked him over. He'd already defended her once. And his clear blue eyes when he looked at her seemed honest and sincere. But could she fully trust him? Would he put her interests above those of his own?

He also had a reputation as a ruthless man. He'd

been known to use force against his enemies. He would do whatever was necessary, she sensed, to get what he wanted.

The arrogant manner he had about his demeanor when he read the will and the cold dismissal of the housekeeper forewarned her that he would not tolerate being disobeyed. He was a magistrate like her dead husband. He had, therefore, power. It would not do to provoke him.

She worried. Would he be unrelenting and forceful if she went against his desires concerning her future? Would he turn out to be like the rest, a self-absorbed villain?

She doubted, but her heart told her to believe in him. It pounded heavily as he looked steadily at her. She wanted him to prove he could be depended upon. But she knew only time would reveal if he resembled every other man who'd interfered in her life or not.

She looked carefully at the handsome Corinthian, trying to discern his sincerity. She shook her head. Heaven help her, she didn't know. It was impossible to tell. She remembered once her old Irish nursemaid saying, "Character is better than wealth." She'd never forgotten the wisdom of it.

How many times had she wished someone would demonstrate their trustworthiness to her? Instead, she'd been repeatedly disappointed, surrounded by toadies who bowed to her elderly husband's wealth.

"It would appear I have no choice," she said at last and removed her hand from his. The contact was broken.

In a firm voice she commented, "I hope, sir, you will keep your word. I have many times been disenchanted by men . . . but perhaps you will continue to astonish and be the person you claim yourself to be."

"Be the person I claim to be," he repeated, clearly amused by her sharp barb. "So, you're disenchanted by men and wish to be astonished? You hope I am not part of some curse you believe has been placed upon you by my sex."

He paused in his reiteration and looked her over in a calculating manner, as if he were weighing his options.

"Madame, may I recommend you wait and see whether I am true to my word or not." he said.

He reminded her of her position. It was clear she had no choice in the matter. She had to accept him. The law was not going to permit her to do otherwise.

"If I am some sort of evil warlock bent upon making your life a cursed misery, you may scheme to remove me."

"How so?" she asked.

"By deciding to remarry, perhaps you can find yourself a nice milquetoast of a man who will do as you desire. You could then take complete control over your life."

She wrinkled her nose in distaste at the thought.

The idea of being leg-shackled to a weak-willed husband held no appeal. She knew such simpering fops would resemble her uncle. And the notion of being married to someone like him was repulsive.

He noticed her reaction and a small smile of satisfaction appeared at the corners of his mouth. He was swaying her to accept him.

"Indeed," he finished smoothly. "If I were you, your ladyship, I would wait before hastily rushing off into another man's arms. You might find yourself embracing a toad, instead of a prince."

Standing over her, he leaned into her ear and whispered enticingly, "Or you might put your trust in me. I might surprise you and be exactly who I say I am. I might be the man who could make all your desires and wishes come true."

The plate shook in her hand as she felt his breath upon her skin and heard the soft words luring her to trust him. Rattled by the nearness of his mouth to her face, she hastily rang the service bell to have the tea tray removed.

Taking a deep breath to clear her thoughts, she said, "It would appear, Master Powers, I have no choice but to do so." She settled on playing the waiting game he suggested. She would soon discover whether he was worthy of her trust or not.

Chapter 3

No longer dogged at every step by Mrs. O'Grady, she thrived in her unfettered freedom. Kathleen began taking unaccompanied walks in the nearby hills. She accepted calls from neighbors her late husband had frowned upon. Then she did something truly daring—she started shopping.

She'd never been able to purchase personal items before. When her uncle had money, he usually spent it on himself, and when he didn't, the shopkeepers refused to give him credit. After she married, her husband declared that the local merchants weren't good enough. He had her clothes ordered from far off London or Paris.

And there had been her constant shadow, Mrs. O'Grady. The glowering housekeeper wrote down every choice she'd made. Later any little pleasure she bought was removed from her bedchamber.

"Far too cheap and frivolous," Mrs. O'Grady would explain when she dared to complain. "You are the wife of a discerning gentleman. His lordship would have a fit if he knew you had that silly trinket in your possession."

Uninhibited shopping was a luxurious adventure. She had not experienced such carefree freedom in years. Like an excited child, she stood before a tray of different toiletry bottles in the village shop trying to decide which to buy.

There were more than half-a-dozen rainbow-colored bottles in front of her, gleaming enticingly. Should she choose by smell or by look? For some of the glass containers in themselves were quite appealing. The cut glass and pretty stoppers made her decision quite difficult.

She kept glancing at her companion, waiting for the

moment when he would tell her she couldn't buy anything. Or the merchant, as had often happened in the past when she lived with her uncle, to quietly whisper in her ear she had no credit and therefore would have to leave . . . but neither occurred.

She turned to the tall dandy, wearing mustard-colored breeches, lounging on a striped glass walking cane. He wore a bemused expression.

Unlike her late husband who had whined bitter complaints from the moment she entered a shop till the moment they left, Beau had been patiently waiting. He was smiling, as if he was actually enjoying the excursion.

"Don't tell me you find none of these to your liking?" he asked. His voice was light with amusement. He picked up one of the bottles and delicately sniffed the fragrance. He put it down and picked up another, examining the cut glass stopper.

"They are all wonderful. I am having difficulty choosing," she confessed. "And I suppose you find all of this to be quite tiresome and now wish to leave."

She prepared to depart. But he stopped her, taking her arm.

"I am in no hurry, Lady Langtry. Besides, not all of these can be that pleasing. Perhaps I can help you eliminate a few?"

He picked up several more bottles until he found one with an extremely strong odor. He smelled it and quickly drew back his head.

"Try this. It's called, *sal volatile*," he suggested.

He placed the stopper beneath her nose. "A mixture of distilled animal elements and perfume, I believe."

"You mean like musk?" she asked and took a whiff. The inside of her nose burned. Tears sprang into her eyes.

She coughed and laughing said, "You've tricked me, sir. That was no perfume, but hartshorn, smelling salts."

"*C'est vrai,*" he admitted cheerfully in French with a grin.

The strong perfume was made from distilled male deer horn shavings and perfume. It created ammonia, the mixture necessary for smelling salts.

"I may be a widow, Master Powers, but I am not yet an elderly matron in need of constant reviving from fainting spells." she said with spirit, and placed the bottle back on the tray.

A pretty, red-colored bottle with petal feet and a crystal stopper caught her eye. She opened it and breathed in a delicate scent. The pleasant odor of essence of roses and something a bit more elusive delighted her senses. She could not quite make out what the other underlying ingredients were.

She placed a small dab on her wrist and sniffed.

"This is quite nice," she said. "But I am not certain what else may be in the fragrance other than roses."

"May I?" he asked and lifted her wrist. He leaned intimately closer. He was near enough for her to smell him. His hair was pomaded and it reminded her of the oriental shop she had once visited with Lord Langtry in Dublin. It was an exotic, yet masculine smell, of citrus and spices.

His guinea-colored head bent a little as he sniffed the perfume, looking up into her eyes as he savored the delicate scent.

"Ah—geranium and jasmine, I do believe," he said. "Delightful."

He did not remove his hold and continued instead to gaze steadfastly at her.

"I would not wish to force my opinion upon you, but you might consider purchasing this," he said. "It is not the scent an old lady would wear. I think you will find many a gentleman unwittingly drawn to you. Even though it appears you have decided to take the veil."

He lightly touched the dark one she was wearing. Ever since her husband's death, she had been wearing dark colors and unbecoming clothes.

"Oh-uh, quite," she agreed.

Her heart tripped as he gently released her. "I believe I will buy it."

Distracted, she nearly dropped the bottle. His remark reminded her why she was draped from head to toe in black. It was conventionally correct to be wearing widow's weeds. But she had another more personal reason for wearing the dark garment. It covered her gold hair. She wasn't conceited, but she was aware that men were tempted to use her beauty for their gain.

She did not want another man to try and tie her to him. She had no wish to be manipulated again. She wanted to hide herself completely from view. If she hid her looks, she reasoned, maybe she would be left alone.

He continued to gaze at her with his devilishly handsome smile. It was most disconcerting to be stared at by the handsome Corinthian. It almost made her wish she hadn't chosen to wear the black bonnet with the ugly veil.

Opening her small beaded reticule to dish out coins to pay the merchant, she realized her heart was drumming a double time rhythm. Could this be attraction she was feeling? Did she want him to be interested in her?

She suddenly felt embarrassed by her whimsical notion. Had he noticed her reaction? And what if he had? Would he take advantage of her? Mock her?

She felt her face flush and raised a hand to one of her heated cheeks. Heavens, she was blushing. She hadn't done that since she was a young girl caught trying on her mother's delicate unmentionables.

She took the wrapped bottle from the merchant, placing it in her reticule. She could not decide which intoxicated her more, the scent, or the nearness of her guardian. The attraction was almost too much to countenance.

Feeling heady with the realization, she said, "I think I shall step outside for a bit, Master Powers. The fumes are beginning to overwhelm me."

"Of course, I shall be with you in a trice," he said and solicitously opened the shop door.

I need to cool down, she told herself. *Or I shall find myself thinking some very unholy thoughts. Ones I very much doubt a nun wearing a veil would indulge in.*

Breathing deeply of the fresh air, she continued her inner monologue. She dismissed the possibility that Beau might fancy her.

What would you think of me, dear sir, if you knew of the effect you have on me? Perhaps you see me only as an aloof widow completely incapable of any passionate feelings?

Ha! I am quite heated by your piercing gaze. Aye, you have no idea how your light touch and kind smile have set my heart a-flutter. It is both wonderful and dreadful at the same time. And for someone who has been deprived of tender feelings for such a long time, it is a veritable feast you offer me.

She had to admit it would be wonderful if he did care a wee bit for her. No one had cared about her since her parents' deaths. If he proved himself to be the man he said he was, she would be honored. Indeed if he took an interest in her beyond that which a guardian has for his ward, it would be an emotionally dizzying experience. He would be placing her in the precarious position of falling in love.

* * *

Beau returned to her side. He held a small oblong

package in his hand. Humming under his breath, he seemed quite pleased with himself.

"This," he said presenting it to her with a small bow, "is for you, Madame."

"Me?" she asked, surprised.

She took it from him and broke the string that was tied around the paper. Opening it, she discovered a silk fan.

"You appeared overheated," he said. "I thought perhaps you would enjoy using this little bit of frippery."

She unfolded it. The fan had mother of pearl stays and a hand painted silk screen. On the shiny fabric was the charming depiction of a young couple walking hand in hand by a tranquil lake.

"Why it's Dovehill!" she exclaimed.

She recognized the view at once. It was the same one she saw daily from her bedchamber window. It was of the lake and the green hills near Dovehill Hall.

Pleased, she waved the fan back and forth, admiring the countryside painted in colors of delicate blue, green, and pale pink. Small woodland creatures frolicked in the foreground and clusters of tiny flowers grew at the couple's feet. The edge of the fan was gilded in painted silver. A tassel of matching color dangled from the pivot, holding the stays together.

"But 'tis far too costly a gift for me to accept, Master Powers," she said, a furrow of doubt creasing her brow.

She recognized the value of the elegant ornamentation. It was a high quality fan. Families usually bought such items for wedding celebrations. They were treasured by the owners as heirloom keepsakes of the event. Often they were kept in cedar-lined chests for preservation.

"Nonsense," he said, dismissing the idea out of hand. "I am not some callow lad attached to his mama's apron strings. This was made to be held in the hands of a beautiful lady. And as you are overheated and quite lovely, it suits you. Thus, you may not refuse my little trifle."

"But I—" she said, wanting to protest. This was not a "little trifle," as he had so elegantly described it. It must have cost a pretty penny.

However, she could not continue. He shook his head and wagged his index finger at her as if she were a young child. She was being naughty. His mind would not be changed. The gift was hers.

She gave a small laugh of concession. It was a beautiful gift. And how could she refuse when he was so pleased to be giving it to her? It would be petty to do so.

"I see now, sir, why you have made yourself quite a reputation as a magistrate. For no barrister would dare argue against you. Indeed you are one of the most decisive gentlemen I have ever had the pleasure to meet."

"Thank you, ma'am, for the compliment. And for the honor of giving you this," he said, lightly tapping the fan.

He was inordinately pleased to see the flush of pink that colored her cheeks. If only he could be the one to help the lovely lady's smile travel from her lips to her sad eyes, he would have accomplished something truly noteworthy.

Looking down at her small black figure troubled him. She was young and had a sparkling character. Like a fine bottle of champagne kept in a dank cellar, she appeared to be wrapping herself in black sadness. And he sensed something else. She was afraid.

He frowned. He could do nothing, he sensed, to dispel that fear. Only time would prove that he was as good as his word. He would slowly have to gain her trust.

*   *   *

"What say you, Madame, of traveling to Dublin with me?" he asked. "I must go there to attend to the other half of the partnership. They require my help in clearing up a few tiresome legal matters at the chambers there."

"I—I do not know," she said, hesitating.

She bit down on her lower lip. Should she leave the safety of Dovehill Hall to live in a bachelor's residence in Dublin town?

She glanced at him. Could he be trusted? Or was she once more to be taken advantage of, to be used like a bargaining chip? To be sold off to the highest bidder to be found in Dublin's salons?

He put a comforting hand on her shoulder.

"I see you are troubled. Perhaps I can ease your worries? There is a sea captain's widow visiting here in the village, do you know of Lady Agnes Fitzpatrick?"

"Yes, I have heard of her," she said. "She is considered to be a veritable paragon of respectability."

She did not add that rumors had been told aplenty concerning the small Irish lady. The widow was known to have taken over the delicate match between her wealthy niece, the Spinster of Brightwood and the eligible bachelor, the Earl of Drennan, with the determination of a dragon protecting its treasure.

"She is the aunt of Lady O'Brien, the lady you and I helped rescue. She is also the widow of Captain Fitzpatrick whose ship and crew mysteriously disappeared somewhere in the darkest part of the uncharted world."

"What do you think of her as a possible companion for yourself? Shall I ask her to accompany us to Dublin and attend upon you?" he asked.

She gave it some thought. Such a formidable lady would help keep her virtue safe, even with a handsome bachelor in residence. And therefore the proprieties would be correctly observed. The intimidating lady would make certain neither he, nor any other gentleman she met, could force his will upon her.

She conjured up in her mind the tiny Irish woman from memory. Lady Fitzpatrick was small in stature, she recalled, but imposing in spirit. The lady was a formidable force to be reckoned with, a veritable whirlwind of determination.

Aye, she decided, the stern sea captain's widow was the perfect solution. She would protect her against any unscrupulous gentleman. Including, she cast a doubtful glance at her guardian, this one.

"Yes, I do believe Lady Fitzpatrick will suit," she said, quickly coming to a decision. "You may send for her straight away." And so it was that the formidable Irish lady was hired as her companion.

Chapter 4

They rode through Dublin's main thoroughfare, Sackville Street, as they headed towards Beau's townhouse. Kathleen looked out of the carriage window at the street before her, admiring the classic whitewashed brick buildings with their wide portico terraces and tall Romanesque facades. The city had a classically elegant air about it. She found the busy town to be quite pleasing.

The abolition of the Irish Parliament due to the 1801 Act of Union with England had prevented some of the older buildings from being demolished. The town was a bit tarnished and outdated. However, it was abuzz with noisy liveliness as they drove through the wide main street.

Men in fox-red British uniforms rode by their carriage on cavalry horses. She noticed poor beggars in rags hold out their hands at passing dandies. Elegant ladies wearing feathered turbans walked in front of trailing maids carrying large packages and wicker baskets on the walkways.

The local Dublin Gazette proudly announced that the town was currently the second largest in the United Kingdom in terms of population and wealth, having over 178,000 souls in its vicinity. It was known as *Baile Atha Cliath* in Gaelic, the town of the hurdle ford. And its fortified seaport had garnered a noteworthy reputation in trade.

From her seat she cast a furtive glance at her new companion. The lady seated across from her was not a normal-sized person. Indeed, Lady Agnes Fitzpatrick was frequently mistaken to be one of the wee people by the more superstitious, but her tiny frame exuded a strong will that was most intimidating. It was a fact that caused the elderly Irish lady to give a derisive laugh, when she dared to remark upon it. "Aye, look at Boney, that French dictator. He's short of stature and yet managed t' crown himself emperor of most of the civilized world. Indeed, 'tis said the smaller the person, the more powerful in character they become. For sure now, my dear Captain used to tell me I was the most interesting lady of his acquaintance. He never wished to see me metamorphosed into a giantess with long limbs and dove like airs. Nay, he liked me just as I am, a tiny lioness."

Lady Fitzpatrick had quickly agreed to accompany her to Dublin for the fortnight. It would provide an excellent opportunity to help her niece, Lady Beatrice, shop for a trousseau as her nuptials to the earl were soon to be held at Drennan Castle.

"And, as ye helped free my Bea' from that despicable villain, I feel it my bound Christian duty to keep your ladyship safely out of temptation's way," the tiny lady said, casting a meaningful look at the guinea-haired Adonis towering over her.

"Aye, even if the devilishly handsome temptation has the inordinate good taste to recommend me to you as your companion."

The tiny woman raised her parasol threateningly. She was a diminutive David ready to fight off a towering Goliath all in the name of moral propriety.

"I shall protect you, Lady Langtry, from wicked men. Indeed, with such a charming face as yours, I shall need to pray to the good Lord above for extra help and guidance. Aye, maybe Saint Laurence will aid my endeavor in chaperoning you, as well," she said, referring to the patron saint who'd once been an archbishop in Dublin. "Or perhaps do me one better."

"In what way do you mean, Lady Fitzpatrick?"

"Why you may be recently widowed and grieving, but surely you know better than t' want to remain in this singular state. It may do very well for someone like me who is old and already lived a full life. But for someone like yourself . . . well, 'tis not suitable. Aye, it would be an aberration against God's divine will for you to live the rest of your life alone. Nay, you shall remarry, my dear," she said with an air of complete certainty. "You may not believe it, but one day you shall."

Kathleen drew back away from her. The idea of marriage was daunting. She had had enough of being controlled. It would take her some time before she could again trust a man.

Noticing her abashed look of horror, the older lady patted her hand.

She said in a comforting manner, "Aye, you are too recently widowed to want to retie the knot . . . one can see that. But given time the idea may hold some appeal. I have traveled from port to port all across this earth looking for news of my missing husband. I am glad to report there are many good gentlemen who travel this planet with us."

Lady Fitzpatrick tilted her head meaningfully towards the window. On the other side, Beau rode with the outriders. He looked quite dashing seated astride a beautiful brown gelding. He rode his mount with ease, a man born to the saddle.

Kathleen had to concede that her guardian was proving himself to be unerringly a gentleman of his word. A fact she had thought would never occur. He didn't disturb her privacy, nor did he try to control or censor her actions. She'd been experiencing unmonitored freedom.

But then she barely knew him. He may in a few weeks' time prove to be full of cunning guile and take advantage of his position as her guardian. He might marry her off like her uncle had and take control of Dovehill Hall.

This dark thought caused her alarm. Secretly, she

wanted him to prove he was an exceptional gentleman. She desired to have one by her side. It would be good to have someone she could depend upon and trust.

Aye, it was lovely having Lady Fitzpatrick as her companion. The older woman was proving herself to be a good friend. But there were lonely moments when she yearned for something more than companionship.

She had witnessed as a child a special loving bond between her parents. And that memory was deeply embedded in her thoughts. She yearned for such caring intimacy. And she knew that only a devoted couple could share that kind of closeness.

* * *

The townhouse was a pleasant surprise. It was situated next to St. Stephen's Green, a place that had once been a medieval enclosure and named after the holy saint who had been stoned to death for preaching Christianity.

The more than twenty acres of trees, lake, and expanses of green lawn within the busy perimeters of Dublin was a welcome respite from busy town life. Around the picturesque green, townhouses and impressive Georgian brick mansions had been built.

A classical Palladian façade with two white columns greeted Kathleen at the front door. The decorative glass over it was shaped in a fanned peacock design. It was a feature unique to Irish townhouses.

Beau opened the door. *"Bienvenue . . .* my younger sister, Laeticia, would normally be here to greet you. But she is at present in London being entertained by friends," he said as they entered the foyer.

At the mention of the young woman, Lady Fitzpatrick gave a sniff of disapproval. She had met the sister. She had not been impressed.

Beau's sister, Laeticia, was a high-stepper with

unbecoming forward manners. The older widow confided to Kathleen later, "That one thinks so highly of herself that if you were to introduce her to the Pope, she'd think he should be kissing her hand! Not the other way around."

"Your sister, she does not act as hostess here?" Lady Fitzpatrick asked Beau in a judgmental tone, running a finger over a sideboard table.

She inspected it for dust. There was none.

"Knowing you may have important business clients to call upon you today, including Lady Langtry, your sister stays away, leaving the head of your table empty?"

"I fear my sister is a headstrong woman, Lady Fitzpatrick. I may ask her to do one thing, and she will go and do quite another. To be truthful, I can barely keep her in hand. She always manages to get her way."

"Humph," murmured Lady Agnes with disdain. "Not very sisterly in loyal devotion then is she? 'Tis no wonder that she is not yet married. No gentleman worth his salt would want to be always reining her in."

She directed her comments in an appraising manner. "Although you are a fine gentleman, Master Powers, one can see that you have a kind heart. Aye, I suppose a weakness such as yours cannot be helped. Orphaned, are the two of ye? No older living relations to help and guide you? No surviving aunt or uncle?"

"No, ma'am. My parents passed away from cholera when I was a student studying at Trinity College. I have no other relative. My sister is my entire family."

"And so you have the sole care and guardianship of her?"

He nodded in affirmation and gave Kathleen a wink. The solicitor reacted to the interrogation in a sporting manner. He appeared to be highly amused by the tiny Irish woman.

Kathleen in turn could not suppress a smile. Lady Agnes was being rude.

And she'd felt a pang of empathy for him when he announced both his parents had died. Like her, Beau and his sister had been orphaned at a tender age. But despite that painful tragedy, he had managed to overcome the loss and gone on to become a successful solicitor. It was an admirable achievement.

She could not help but wonder what her life would have been like if she had had someone like him to watch over her, instead of being bartered away by her greedy uncle into an unwanted marriage with an aged lord.

Would she have led a carefree life full of parties and friends like Laeticia? No. She somehow knew instinctively that she would not have been as extreme as Laeticia was. Even so, it was difficult not to feel a sharp pang of envy at the thought.

"A grand shame . . . you've indulged your sister's whims too much. She is quite spoiled, and at twenty-one dangerously nearing spinsterhood," said the old widow decisively.

Kathleen blanched a little at the older woman's blunt manner. She was not holding back her opinions. And being as she was Irish, Lady Agnes had a sharp tongue and was using it like a double-edged sword.

To a stranger her ladyship's forthrightness was a bit unsettling. But her friends knew her loyalty was fixed. It never changed, meriting an equal devotion from those upon whom she bestowed it. She was feisty, it was true, but it was not difficult to like the tiny spitfire.

"Faith, it is no wonder then that your sister makes like a vagabond and does what she wishes, and goes wherever she chooses. Ah, well . . . I suppose I ought to be grateful for that. She'll not be underfoot while we're here. Indeed I shall enjoy watching over this gentle lady. Aye, and if you're wondering if ye had asked me to chaperone that willful sister of yours, I tell you plain, sir, I'd have bluntly refused."

Kathleen turned to Beau expecting a sharp reaction, but he sallied back at the petite virago before him, maintaining his usual calm with a touch of wry humor.

"Oh, uh—quite," said Beau, but then a glimmer of dry amusement entered his voice. "For I suppose if she were here, Laeticia might accidentally step on some respectable toes, and we mustn't have that, must we? After all, a young lady should only desire to please her elders and not herself when looking for a spouse, and any thoughts of her attending balls and meeting eligible young gentlemen who might want to marry her . . . well, that would be quite unpardonable."

"Enough," muttered the tiny Irish woman, interrupting him with a pounding of the tip of her parasol against the marble floor. "I see what you're getting at, young man. You think that high-stepping sister of yours can manage well enough on her own, without any guidance from someone more experienced, such as myself."

"Indeed."

"Humph," answered the tiny lady, conceding the point. "I suppose she'll make do, as I recall that chit did have a few winsome ways about her, which some gentlemen might find to be appealing. Aye, and as I have enough to occupy myself with this gentle lady here . . ."

She gave a pointed glance at Kathleen who was observing the conversation with wide-eyed wonder. She had never seen two people speak to each other with such vigor and yet maintain their good humor. It was quite a wonder.

"I'll therefore not take any further offense at her rude absence," concluded the spirited companion.

"That is most magnanimous of your ladyship to do so," Beau agreed. Smiling, he gave a small bow of acknowledgment of the truce between them.

The whole exchange made Kathleen a bit wistful. It was refreshing to see Lady Fitzpatrick and Master

Powers banter in this way, sallying words back and forth, without any fear of negative repercussions.

She'd remembered her parents had talked in this lively manner when they were alive. Their conversations at times had been quite witty. But at the same time respectful, not dismissive. Unlike the conversations she'd had with her late husband, who always made her feel foolish and naive.

She suddenly wished she could make Beau smile and laugh at something she said . . . She caught herself in mid-thought, but then maybe he was only trying to win Lady Agnes over in order to maintain her goodwill?

She frowned. She looked over the handsome solicitor and reminded herself to keep her guard up. Perhaps his sunny disposition would change?

Her uncle had been kind to her in the beginning, as well, but in due time he had become cold-hearted and self-centered. Eventually, he'd ceased to take care of her altogether . . . and she continued to worry that her new guardian might do the same.

Hiding a grin, Beau turned, and spied a gentleman he himself depended upon—his valet. The servant approached them and bowed to the ladies as way of greeting. The slightly pepper-haired gentleman with the build of a pugilist, whispered discreetly into his master's ear.

Beau murmured, "I see . . . Ladies, may I present to you, Humphrey Whitfield, my man. He will show you to your rooms. My housekeeper, Mrs. Robinson, has stepped out to attend to some shopping. Apparently, she only received word this morning of our impending arrival. Laeticia had apparently forgotten to inform her." He stopped what he was about to say next. He frowned and glanced at the tiny Irish widow.

Lady Fitzpatrick raised her eyebrows meaningfully.

He did not need to continue. What he had to say only proved what the chaperone had already said to be true. His sister was thoughtless, as well as spoiled.

A proper hostess would have planned ahead, and she would have informed the servants of their coming. Then, upon their arrival, she would have been there to politely greet them at the door and invite them into the drawing-room. They would have been served a welcoming dish of hot tea and scones. But none of that expected hospitality had come to pass.

Beau's sister, too preoccupied with her own plans, had not troubled herself with anyone else's. She had not bothered to inform the servants of their impending arrival, placing those in service in an uncomfortable position. They were not ready for their master and his guests' arrival. Her behavior was most inconsiderate and self-centered. Two character faults that now could not be overlooked with good humor and a quip.

Humphrey helped the outriders carry their trunks up to the bedchambers. He returned and guided them around the house. Their chamber windows faced Saint Stephen's Green. And as she looked out, Kathleen enjoyed the sight of the lush trees and strolling pedestrians.

"At least the housekeeper knows her business," commented Lady Fitzpatrick, sticking her head into the room. "The curtains are well shaken and I've noticed the chambermaid has swept what ash there was out of the fire grates. There is even fresh paper and pens on the writing desks. It would appear the young mistress of the house may be lacking in preparedness, but not the servants. Aye, those serving here appear to be well devoted to their duties. He is a fortunate man to have such good service."

Kathleen nodded in agreement, looking at the well-kept room.

The large four-poster bed was not as grand as the one she had at Dovehill Hall. The poles were shorter and less heavy in stature. But they suited the room's size. The bed linens were made up of white cotton damask with a colorful pattern of leaves and flowers loomed on Jacquard machinery. The manufactured fabric had recently come into popularity, being vastly cheaper than those loomed by hand.

The window and bed draperies were made of cherry-red merino fabric. The material was a mixture of thin woolen-twilled cloth combined with spun silk. It was very fashionably cut and looped on the Grecian-styled window rods.

"One cannot fault Master Powers's taste," she said, touching the curtains' long fringes. The house reflected the gentleman's style. It was elegant and tasteful. Displaying none of the ornate, over-the-top decorating her late husband had spent Midas amounts of time and money upon.

"Indeed," her companion agreed, looking at the young widow thoughtfully, "he does . . . Come, my dear, I believe a cup of tea is what is called for now. The dust from our journey still lies thickly in the back of my throat, and I want to see if the food served is equally as pleasing as the decor."

* * *

It was as they were entering the salon a loud commotion was heard outside. The sounds of an angry man yelling and the loud barking of a dog penetrated the stone walls of the townhouse.

Curious, Kathleen opened the front door.

Barking, while trying to escape the man chasing after him, was a large black beast that bounded past the front door. Two paws the size of large saucers planted themselves on Kathleen's shoulders. A long, rough tongue proceeded to joyfully lick her face.

"Down," commanded a stern voice from nearby.

Beau pulled off her what now appeared to be a large puppy. The animal obediently complied, his long tail wagging.

"Ye damnable son of Lucifer!" yelled a man in an oily cap coming up the portico steps. "Get out of there. I'm gonna whip your black hide until you're dead this time. That'll be the last time you run away from me— you worthless bit of flea-bitten fur!"

The animal, upon seeing the angry man, growled. The hair on the back of its thick neck bristled. His large puppy eyes squinted in anger.

Compassionately, Kathleen bent down and put her arms around the animal's neck, trying to soothe him.

"It's all right, boy, no one is going to harm you," she said reassuringly, looking up at Beau for agreement.

"Here, give me back m' dog," demanded the man gruffly.

"How much?" said Beau, crisply.

"How much for what?" repeated the stranger.

He reached his hand out to grab the dog, but the animal bared its fangs at him. Cautiously, he drew back.

"The dog—I wish to purchase him from you," Beau reiterated.

"Now see here, Gov'—that animal belongs t' me. I can do with him what I likes."

"I did not say otherwise," Beau said, removing a few shillings from his waist pocket. "I wish to purchase him from you."

"He's been nothing but trouble. Eating me out of house and home, running off every chance he gets . . ." the man said.

His thunder slowed as Beau placed coin after coin into his outstretched hand. When five shillings were placed into his palm, the man stopped his mutterings.

He counted the coins out one by one and said, not giving the animal a second glance, "But seeing as your lady here seems taken with him . . . well, for sure now, I suppose I could part with the troublesome beast."

As if sensing his change in fortune, the dog began to once again vigorously wag his tail. He rubbed his large black head up against her hand.

She stroked him. She'd always liked animals. They were never greedy and never betrayed you. They simply wanted to be fed and taken care of.

After the oily man had parted, Beau asked her, "What name shall you give him, Lady Langtry? He's yours now."

This announcement was a surprise. She had not expected him to give her the dog. She had thought he would have wanted to keep the animal for himself, since he had paid for him. But from the broad smile he'd bestowed upon her, she could see that he was pleased to do so.

She smiled her thanks, and petting the animal gave its name some thought. She said, "I shall call him Tim . . . after Saint Timothy."

"A good name. I hope he is as devoted to you as his namesake was to his master."

Smiling at the young dog, she said with confidence, "He will be."

"Master Powers," said Lady Fitzpatrick, warily eyeing the puppy, which stood as tall as her shoulders. "I do hope you have a barn attached to this domicile."

"I do. Why, Lady Fitzpatrick?"

"Because this creature you think is a dog, by the looks of him, might turn out to be a horse."

"Then I shall buy a saddle and you will have to ride him if he is," put in Kathleen with a hint of a laugh.

"Hmm . . ." The tiny lady nodded, eyeing the puppy up and down. "We shall have to check it for fleas." With a decisive nod, she walked into the parlor. They followed her in, the expected tea waiting for them on a serving tray.

[67]

* * *

Days at St. Stephen's Green passed pleasantly with visits to art galleries, concert halls, and excursions to the center of Dublin, as well as to places of note, such as Saint Patrick's Cathedral. It was that pulpit Jonathan Swift, the author of *Gulliver's Travels*, had once served as dean and was now entombed in.

Kathleen had begun to take early morning promenades on the green with Tim loping along beside her on his large clumsy paws. Her chaperone, Lady Agnes, on occasion, would absent herself in order to help Lady Beatrice, her niece, with buying items for her upcoming nuptials. She carried around in her reticule a long list containing items her niece requested. The bride was about to become mistress of the newly renovated Drennan Castle and needed to replace many outdated household items.

Master Powers would spend most of his day in court. He worked at helping sort out matters at the partnership, meeting clients, and other members of chambers. His expertise was invaluable to the solicitors. As a result, she seldom saw him until evening.

"Come on, boy," she called to Tim, who stood on the green, gazing at the waterfowl. The birds were floating in the duck pond connected to the River Liffey. "No swimming today."

She'd been teaching him to come and to fetch with an old croquet ball. The large square in front of the townhouse had proved to be the perfect patch of wide lawn for letting the young animal frolic. When Beau had a moment to spare, he would help her train him.

They had come to the conclusion that Tim was a mixed breed. He was part Labrador with a smattering of Irish setter. His large paws and black head bespoke of his parentage. He proved at first to be an unruly creature, tearing into bedchamber slippers and sneaking food off the kitchen table. However, with consistent and stern disciplining, he was turning into a well-behaved pet.

She admired the firm voice Beau used in telling the dog to "stay."

Tim obediently did not budge. His tail wagged happily while he sat, not moving, knowing his master would soon release him to run across the green.

"I wonder," she offhandedly remarked, "if children can be as easily trained."

Beau gave a small laugh at the thought.

"I rather doubt it. If I recall, my poor nurse often told me that she was at wit's end as to what to do with me," he confessed. "I am afraid I was a little demon. I often caused trouble. And no amount of threats or reprimands had any effect on me."

"So what changed you?" she asked, trying to picture this disciplined gentleman as an impish boy looking for a mischievous lark.

"School," he said with a sigh. "The discipline of an all boys' parochial school should never be dismissed."

"Oh, dear," she said with a nod of understanding. For it was well-known how rigid such institutions of conservative education could be.

"I suppose it is why I am overly indulgent with my sister," he confessed, sheepishly. "I was like her when I was a lad."

In that moment she could picture him as a father. He would laugh and play with his children, and when needed, discipline them. She imagined he would be a very fair-minded parent, having once been a little troublemaker himself. At that thought she unknowingly gave him a smile of approval, causing his heart to skip a beat.

She tried to copy Beau's disciplinary manner, but to no avail. The pup had cast her in the role of adopted mother. She was there to pet, feed, and take him for his daily walks, not to discipline him.

Once, when she was angry at Tim for chasing one of the green's geese, instead of coming when called, she used a harsh tone with him. The dog reluctantly came, giving her a brown-eyed look of reproach.

He seemed to silently say, "How can you yell at me for doing my duty of chasing off that nasty bird? Didn't you hear it honk insults at me?" And for the remainder of the day, he sulked under his favorite chair.

Today, the puppy was behaving perfectly. He came obediently to her side when she called, his tail happily wagging.

They crossed Carlisle Bridge, the stone footpath traversing the River Liffey, which connected to a small lake. It was unusually empty. The pedestrians who routinely used the green had stayed indoors as a cool morning haze enveloped it.

A mallard squawked and took flight, off the water to their right. Its green wings fluttered as it changed position. Tim began to growl.

"I'll have none of that," she said to him firmly, gripping his leash more tightly. "We are not chasing birds today. After this walk you shall have a biscuit with a bit of gravy and I shall have a warming cup of tea."

But the young dog did not appear to pay attention. He continued to give a throaty murmur of discontent.

They walked across the stone bridge. The occasional sound of quacking ducks and fluttering wings could be heard below.

Tim's growl grew louder. It was not directed at her or the waterfowl below, but at a group of trees off in the near distance. He refused to move. The hair on the back of his neck bristled. His large paws dug stubbornly into the stone.

"It's all right, Tim, there's no one here. Just us, lad,"

she said reassuringly, pulling on his leash.

But it did no good. He barked at the swaying branches ahead on the side of the path. It was then she saw the long end of a gun's barrel aimed at her.

She started to turn away, but it was too late. She heard the loud crack of gunfire.

Losing her balance as Tim suddenly leaped forward, she fell roughly onto her hands and knees. She could feel the hard stones beneath. Her skin rubbed against the unforgiving surface.

Smoke emitted into the air from the fired shot. The bullet zipped past, flying wide towards the ducks. Frightened by the loud report, the birds took flight off in a circular pattern into the hazy sky.

The shooter fired again.

This time, the bullet hit the stone railing above her head. A spray of shattered fragments fell. Frantic, no longer obeying commands, Tim rushed towards the trees and the hidden gunman.

The leash slipped through her fingers.

Lying prone, afraid of moving lest the shooter try again, she heard a man yell, "Get off me . . . damn dog!"

Looking up, she watched a man appear from behind the screen of tree branches. He ran from the footpath. With the gray mist heavy in the air, she could not identify the man. He was a fog-blurred figure.

Hurriedly, she arose and chased after them. Frightened, she called frantically, "Tim . . . Tim . . . come here, boy!"

The layers of her skirts and petticoats caused her to trip and stumble as she rushed to get to Tim. Her heart pounded heavily—she worried for her pet's safety, rightly reasoning the villain might have shot the puppy.

She heard a loud yelp and hastened forward.

Lying on the green was Tim. He'd been bludgeoned on the head by the end of the firing pistol. Blood trickled from his skull.

She knelt, touching the unconscious dog. Nothing appeared to be broken. Frightened, she looked about. The gunman was nowhere to be seen. He'd run off.

"Oh, Tim," she whispered as she ran her hand over his black fur.

Kneeling by the brave dog, tears of regret welled in her eyes. If only she'd held on more tightly to his leash, this would never have happened. He'd been trying to protect her.

She took off her long gabardine cloak, realizing the animal was too heavy to carry, and covered him. She rose and ran back to the house to seek help.

Kathleen had no idea what state she was in when she rushed into the study where Beau was quietly reading. Her hair and clothes were in complete disarray, the walking gown torn and shredded. At the sight of splattered blood on her clothes and hands, his heart nearly stopped beating.

He hurried to her side, exclaiming, "What's happened! Are you wounded?"

He took her into his arms, feeling her limbs, reassuring himself that she was not physically harmed. He could feel her heart thumping loudly against his chest as her body trembled from shock.

She tried to regain her composure to speak. She said shakily, "No-o . . . I'm fine. But Tim . . . he's been badly hurt." And she proceeded to explain what had occurred.

Upon learning of the terrible events that had taken place, Beau, with a look of deadly determination, opened a locked case. Inside, neatly aligned by size, were his shooting pistols.

Humphrey appeared by his side.

"May I be of service, sir?"

"Aye, load these for me," he said, choosing two weapons.

He kept glancing over at her, as if he was reassuring

himself that she was truly alive and unharmed.

Methodically, with the expertise of a man used to dealing with such crises, the valet chose ammunition and checked the weapons' mechanisms. This was not the first time his master had called him into such service. Master Powers's actions always matched his words. This was a man for whom his word was his bond. He was someone others could count upon in times of danger.

The guns were laid on the table. Beau picked them up and holstered them beneath his cloak. He turned to her.

"I want you to stay here. That madman may be still lurking about. He might try to harm you again."

'No," she said, shaking her head. "I want to go with you. Tim is my dog and he was hurt trying to protect me. I want to be there for him, to help if I can."

"Very well," he agreed, his eyes sparkling with admiration.

She stood before him anxious for her pet, but she'd not gone into a fit of hysterics, or played the part of a frightened damsel in distress. She was eager, ready to brave the possibility of once again meeting the villain who tried to shoot her. She was truly a remarkable woman.

"But you are to stay behind me. You are too tempting a target for this madman to resist."

She quickly agreed and they hastened back to the bridge.

Upon arriving at the spot where she'd left the dog, a constable on patrol was standing over the unconscious animal. He looked at them, noticing their winded conditions and anxious looks.

Nodding at the pup, he asked, "This lad yours?"

"Yes, Officer," she answered, hurrying over to her pet.

She was pleased to see Tim half-open his eyes. Relief flooded her. He was alive.

Beverly Adam

Spying the large firing pistols hidden inside Beau's overcoat, the constable's face grew stern.

"For sure now, you're not thinking of putting the animal down, are ye, sir? He's a young lad and from the looks of him, he's been badly treated. But he's not in such a terrible condition that ye must be rid of him. Aye, all he needs is some rest."

The constable drew himself up to his full height. He tapped his walking stick into his hand. "Also, I won't let you fire off those weapons. This is a public place and you might accidentally shoot someone."

Beau drew back.

The idea he would ever harm a family pet, let alone have the temerity to shoot off a weapon without due reason, was clearly an insulting suggestion.

"I am a gentleman, sir," he said, in a clipped tone. "I do not run around killing brave dogs who've been bludgeoned by a cowardly villain. Nor do I carry firearms on my person for mere sport. That would be quite beneath me. Not to mention reprehensibly caddish behavior. Now, if you don't mind, Constable, I should like to take the dog home."

Without further ado, he picked up the unconscious pup and quickly walked towards the townhouse. His long legs strode across the green in record time. Kathleen and the startled constable followed at a half-trot behind.

Humphrey promptly opened the front door when they returned. He'd dutifully stood by the front window anticipating their arrival. While they were gone, the housekeeper had placed a pile of old blankets by the hearth fire.

One of the chambermaids cooed over the young animal as he was brought in. "Oh—you're a wonderful brave dog, ye are, Tim."

Hearing his name, the dog opened his eyes. He gave

[74]

a soft whimper of pain. Everyone exclaimed, telling him what a brave creature he was, anxious that he be made comfortable by the hearth.

As if sensing he was once again in a safe place, the animal went limp in his master's arms. His eyes closed as he became unconscious.

"To think such disturbing events should happen here," said the constable in disbelief after being informed of what had taken place.

Glancing about the bachelor's townhouse, the officer gave the young woman a shrewd look. "You certain you'll be safe here, ma'am? Do ye have any relations in town with whom you might wish to stay?"

She thought briefly of her uncle. But the notion of contacting him would be as if she were inviting herself to relive a nightmare.

A huff of indignation was uttered beside her.

Lady Fitzpatrick, who'd recently returned from shopping for her niece, bristled. Her parasol's stays quivered in her hand. She would have struck the man in front of her or anyone else who might have stood in her way, if provoked.

"Her ladyship has her guardian to look after her, Constable," Lady Agnes said with all the stiff indignation she could muster. "And I have many a time stared down pirates and unruly mutineers. As for Lady Langtry's relations, I shouldn't put it past one of the worthless cur to have tried to end her life. She is a lady of substantial means and I am quite certain not one of them would mind if she should suddenly have an untimely demise. They may have possibly arranged this cowardly ambush! If I were you, Constable, I would check into their present whereabouts."

"I think that would be a waste of valuable time, ma'am," said the constable, doubtfully.

Rather than contemplating the notion of a greedy

relative with a nefarious motive, it was evident the constable thought a pistol-shooting lunatic was running around the green. The cad was having a bit of sadistic fun frightening the young lady and her pet. That he had struck the young animal had been nothing less than unfortunate.

"I better gather up a few of my lads and make a thorough search of the green. The villain may still be lurking about. Good day, ladies," he said.

Tipping his hat, he left without bothering to address the master of the house, recalling the way that haughty gentleman had looked coldly at him. It had sent shivers down his spine. For sure now, he had no doubt that if the gun-shooting lout was caught, either the tiny lady or the imposing dandy would see him neatly planted in the ground. He almost pitied the lunatic who'd dared to frighten the young woman and her pet.

After the constable left, Beau said, "I shall personally go to the chief of police and see that a further investigation is undertaken. I do not believe this was a random act of violence. The shots that were aimed at Kathleen were premeditated. I am certain of it. The villain intended on killing her."

He did as he promised, but nothing became of it. All of Kathleen's relatives had impeccable alibis as to the day in question. As for the villain who had shot at Kathleen, he escaped into the mist, which angered Beau. He became determined that Kathleen be well-protected.

"What did the police say?" she asked when he returned from the police station. It was now raining outside and droplets fell from his clothes.

She could tell by his grim face that the news was not good. Comfortingly, she bent down and petted Tim who lay near the fire recuperating.

Beau knew the only ones to gain from Kathleen's death were her greedy in-laws and her cad of an uncle.

At the reading of the will, he'd felt their palpable hatred of her, the one person who stood between them and a mountain of wealth

"They won't listen to me," he said, exasperated. "I'm almost certain a member of your family tried to have you shot and killed. That sneering countess and her overfed son, Henry . . . I wouldn't put it past them to make a try. They had more reason than anyone to believe that with you dead, they would inherit Dovehill Hall and all its holdings."

He frowned. "Indeed, that hungry cad of an uncle of yours could have been behind this. Any of them could've hired someone to have you killed and out of the way." He angrily tossed a small twig into the fire. "But without any concrete evidence, the law refuses to do anything."

"What do you intend to do?"

He crouched down and took her hand. His was cold from being outside, as it had rained, but hers warmed him clear to his heart.

He could see the worry in her wide blue eyes, but her back was straight and her shoulders set. She was a brave young woman and had already been through enough in her young life. It tore him a little to see her this way. She may have once been a married woman, but she was still young and unknowing of the world, living as she had, imprisoned in that gloomy place by her heartless husband.

"I will protect you," he said.

"How?"

"By remaining by your side, guarding you from any harm, along with Humphrey's help. We must be vigilant until all of this is sorted out and the villains are brought to justice."

"That may take a while," she said. "And you may grow tired of protecting me. I've had visits from several ladies of Dublin society who'd like nothing better than the presence of your company . . ." She nodded towards a stack of calling cards, leaving unsaid that he was much in demand. "I think you might become quickly bored watching over me all the time."

She thought about how almost every notorious Irish actress and high-stepping debutante with their mamas and companions in tow had come to pay a visit since they'd arrived in Dublin.

"Kathleen, nothing at the moment matters more to me than your protection."

"Truly?"

"Truly." The minute he uttered the words, he knew he meant it. She'd become more than a duty he had to fulfill. He genuinely cared about her. She was different from any other lady of his acquaintance, fresh and vibrant, and wholly attractive.

He bent down and tilting his head, captured her lips with his own. It was a warm, ardent kiss that shot a surge of awareness through her, causing her to grip the arms of her chair. She'd never felt anything like it. Her late husband had always roughly forced her.

Her tongue began to entwine with Beau's, the kiss deepening, as he gently held her head, blood rushing through her . . . until suddenly he drew back, unexpectedly breaking their connection.

"I shouldn't have done that," he said, his voice rough with regret. He shook his head. "You're such an innocent. I . . . I have no right to take advantage of you this way."

"But I liked the kiss."

He laughed. "I liked it too . . . but, I'm having trouble, my dear, keeping my hands off of you."

"But—"

"You are my ward. And despite being a widow, you are inexperienced. As a gentleman, I have no right to take advantage of you this way. I am, as you pointed out, a rogue . . . however, it would appear I am not completely without scruples where you are concerned." He smiled and kissed her hand.

"I see," she said, nodding, feeling a sudden, unexplainable loss. He was being a gentleman. Something she wasn't used to.

However, she wondered, touching her still tingling lips, *what would happen if our kissing had continued? Where would it have led?* She could not help but wonder if perhaps she could somehow entice him into kissing her again. But before she could speak, Lady Fitzpatrick entered the room with her needlepoint and sat down next to her with a harrumph and a pointed look that said she knew something had occurred in her absence. Kathleen sighed and sat back in her chair. What she'd wanted to suggest to him would have to wait for another day.

Chapter 5

While she played on the harp in the drawing-room, Kathleen observed Beau at work. He was sitting at the writing desk inking his quill.

His guinea-colored hair shone in the sunlight streaming in from the front window. In his red brocade vest, white shirtsleeves, and collar decorated with an elegant black cravat, he looked every inch the gentleman magistrate.

He'd been most vigilant and protective since the shooting and carried a loaded revolver whenever they left the house. He was insistent either Lady Fitzpatrick or Humphrey walk by her side, taking extra precautions when he was not able to accompany her himself.

She was never left alone. Always, she was followed by someone. Constantly, she was watched.

Accidentally, she struck a discordant chord on the harp.

Her arched eyebrows wrinkled. She frowned at the unpleasant sound coming from her instrument, contemplating her present situation. It did not sit well.

All this mollycoddling was stifling. It reminded her of her previous oppressive life, when her every step had been dogged and recorded by the dour housekeeper, Mrs. O'Grady. She thought she was finished with that restrictive life, but she was wrong.

She was helpless. And there was nothing she could do to change the situation. Although it would have been easy to do, she could not place any blame on Beau. As her guardian he was trying to protect her.

She'd been shot at and her pet harmed. He was right to be concerned. Only time now would prove she was not some assassin's intended target. She had to be patient.

Filling in the quiet, a soft sigh was heard from Tim. The young dog was sleeping nearby. His long plumed tail stuck out from beneath his favorite chair to inform them of his presence. The brave creature had slowly over the past few days been recovering from the attack. Although the entire household had wanted to give Tim the choicest of food scraps, the animal's stomach would not permit it. He sometimes whined piteously in pain—unable to eat.

She'd taken him that morning, with stalwart Humphrey accompanying them, for his first walk away from the house since the incident. When they crossed the bridge, Tim had growled at the vacant trees and given them the honor of his personal watering.

Beau looked up from his writing, noticing her bored expression.

He put his quill down. After carefully sanding his letter, he said, "Sink me, but your face, Lady Langtry, it's wordlessly proclaiming an unmentionable woe. Don't tell me the doldrums of these last few days has brought this about? Especially after all the excitement you and Tim experienced, one would think you'd be happy with all this quiet living."

"I . . . that is . . ." She could not explain. She felt ashamed.

After she had escaped being shot and possibly killed . . . how could she complain of this new gilded prison? It was carefully crafted for her personal comfort and protection. She was very much indebted to him. She was fortunate to be safely living in his home unharmed.

"Good news," he said cheerfully. "Your unsaid wish is about to come true. We are invited to a dinner party by a naval acquaintance of mine. It is to honor his recent promotion to the rank of captain. I thought you might enjoy a change of scenery, so I've decided to accept the invitation."

He turned to the older woman sitting by the hearth fire. Lady Fitzpatrick had been quietly needle-pointing a canvas of roses onto a piece of fabric. She paused in her work to listen to his announcement.

"That is, Lady Fitzpatrick, if you and Lady Langtry would care to accompany me? I know Lady Kathleen is in mourning, but I think her age might excuse her from becoming a complete recluse, don't you? As it is a rather small dinner party, surely no one will object."

"I agree with you, Master Powers. And it will be my pleasure to accept," replied Lady Agnes, pleased. "Perhaps I will run into an old acquaintance? My husband and I were frequently invited to admirals' tables. They respected Captain Fitzpatrick. He was such an excellent merchant seaman. And for sure now, many an officer was invited to come aboard The Blue Star to dine with us."

"Excellent," he said approvingly. "And you, Lady Langtry? Will you also attend? I think this will be the cure for whatever was causing that dreadful frown you were wearing earlier."

"Yes," she said smiling, already planning what to wear.

Although she was forced to wear black, she felt a happy tingle of anticipation. It would be her first time dressing for a dinner party since her husband's death. Now she would be able to do so without having either her husband or Mrs. O'Grady choosing her gown. The choice would be hers alone.

In her mind she visited her clothes' press. She had three black evening gowns. One was made of crepe, another of bombazine, and a third of velvet. The latter she decided might suit such an intimate setting. She did not think her brown silk was yet suitable to wear as she was still in full mourning.

The next evening she pulled the velvet gown out of

her armoire. She smiled. It had been made by a local dressmaker and had a few Irish flourishes—a style her late husband and the housekeeper would have frowned upon. They would have considered it to be too Irish, and therefore, too inferior to wear.

Happily, fashion had changed within the last few years. Sheer cottons had fallen out of favor after causing legions of thinly dressed women to suffer from unseemly runny noses and constant chills. The heavy black velvet was more than appropriate for the small celebration, and it would keep her warm.

Long sleeves were currently the rage. Hers were ribbon split at the shoulders with white underpinnings, reminding her of a painting she had seen of a young Juliet standing on her balcony. The bodice was elaborately decorated in silver threads, embroidered in a simple Celtic pattern.

"Very nice, m' dear," commented Lady Agnes, as she entered the room to see what her charge had chosen. "Most appropriate for tonight's small *soiree*. What jewels do you plan to wear?"

She picked up her favorite brooch and showed it to her. It was the one she had found on the altar.

"I thought to wear it with a long scarf."

"And what about this?" asked the widow, discreetly pointing to the open square bodice. "Your bosom will be on display. And you are not yet out of mourning."

"I have this," she said, picking up a white fichu insert. "Once tucked inside, it should screen that part of my body. Sadly, I left most of my jewelry back at Dovehill."

She did not add since her husband's death she had not worn the heavy pieces. They reminded her all too well of him. The larger the gem, the heavier the setting of gold or silver, the more it suited Lord Langtry's exhibitionist tastes.

The jewels her late husband had given her held no sentimental value. She had no regrets about not wearing them. She had been merely his dress-up doll. He'd used her to display his wealth, wanting other men to openly envy him.

"But that is not all you have," said the older lady, a twinkle in her brown eyes. She presented her charge with a wooden box. It was made of cedar, inlaid with mother of pearl and delicately crafted by hand.

"It's for you, from Master Powers. There is, I believe, a note enclosed."

Kathleen opened the lid.

"Heavens," she exclaimed, upon looking inside. The gift was exquisite. Nestled on a piece of dark blue silk was a long necklace with a precious gem.

She took it out carefully. Hanging on a string of pearls was a light blue sapphire encircled by small diamonds. The sapphire reflected the candlelight, throwing little starbursts off the walls of the bedchamber.

It quite took her breath away. She had never seen such a finely crafted necklace before. It was exquisite.

"How enchanting," said Lady Agnes, "It matches exactly the color of your eyes. You must wear it tonight. That would so please Master Powers. And it suits you, my dear, to perfection. Ah, there is, as I thought, a note."

She fished out a small envelope and passed it to her.

Breaking the wax seal, Kathleen opened it. She pulled out a small sheath of paper and read the message:

The jewel most fair is the jewel most rare . . .
you.

Dear Kathleen, may this simple token show you how pleased I am that you are accompanying me tonight. It would bring me great pleasure if you would accept this small gift.

As always, your humble servant,
Master Powers.

She blushed, remembering their briefly shared kiss. "It would appear he is more than a wee bit taken with you," said Lady Agnes knowingly. "And the kind gentleman has given me a gift as well . . . God bless him."

She pointed to a gold brooch pinned to her bodice. It was a miniature sailing ship. Its billowing sails were made of mother of pearl. Gold threads were strung from its masts with a diamond point inlaid at the bow.

"What a charming piece," Kathleen remarked approvingly.

She felt added warmth towards Beau for giving Lady Langtry a gift. It was thoughtful of him to bestow one upon the elderly companion.

"It quite suits you, Lady Fitzpatrick."

"Aye, 'tis appropriate for a sea captain's widow," the lady agreed, taking a quick look in the mirror at the both of them. A wistful look passed over her face as she touched the miniature craft.

It was obvious the devoted widow was thinking of her late husband and of the happy times they had shared together onboard his ship. Unshed tears glimmered in her sad eyes.

Kathleen placed a consoling hand on her friend's shoulder and said, "Aren't we a pair?"

Wiping away the tears, the older widow nodded.

She said with a weak smile, "Aye, we are that, but tonight we shall valiantly be the merry widows of Dublin, won't we, my dear?"

"That we shall," agreed Kathleen, noticing her companion had chosen to wear a simple crepe gown with long mutton sleeves and a high-necked bodice.

"At my age," Lady Agnes had told the dressmaker, "it would be unseemly to expose my bosom. And as I do not have a swan's neck that a poet like Lord Byron could wax fanciful upon, I prefer my wrinkles to be covered."

The only part of the widow's gown that had any ornamentation was the hem. It was trimmed with large black roses and a ruffle of silk. The overall effect was discreet elegance and perfectly suitable for a lady of advanced years.

"Faith now, we have the clothes and the finery to wear to tonight's little party. Indeed, you shall look most fetching wearing that gown and necklace," Lady Fitzpatrick commented. "I think your guardian will be most pleased. We shall not bring him shame."

"Most assuredly not," she agreed and had the maid help her place the necklace around her neck.

She could not help but admire how well it suited her. The jewel lying at her throat complemented her coloring and as she looked in the mirror, her blue eyes seemed to sparkle with happy pleasure.

Her efforts with her attire were well rewarded by the admiring look Beau gave her when he saw her. He stood in the foyer beneath the chandelier dressed in black evening attire, waiting to escort them to the dinner party.

She didn't have to ask if he approved of how she looked, she could tell from the admiring light in his blue eyes that he did. His eyes lingered on the jewel lying at her throat for a moment and then upon her smiling face.

"Beautiful," he said softly as he looked into her eyes.

"Yes, it is," she agreed, gently touching the jewel, thinking of how much it must have cost and the trouble he had taken to obtain it.

She added a little shyly, "Thank you. The necklace is so lovely, Beau."

"You are most welcome, but it's not the gem I was speaking of," he replied. Taking her hand, he possessively placed it in the crook of his arm and led them outside to the waiting carriage.

The dinner party was held in a rented townhouse near Dublin Port. It was to be served at the unusually late hour of half-past-six, instead of four. The number of guests, they were told, consisted of a small party of eight.

The carriage drew up to a brick townhouse located not far from the largest sea harbor in Ireland. The party's company was in a celebratory mood, as many of the guests had arrived in advance of them. Outbursts of laughter, song, and piano forte music were heard coming from the drawing-room upstairs.

The room was not very large, but it was pleasantly inviting decorated in a cheerful jonquil yellow and trimmed with a white wainscot boarder. A toasty fire flickered in the black and white marble fireplace located on the left wall. Over it hung an elegant mirror done in the French style of gilded silver, reflecting the golden lights of the wall sconces around the room.

Lady Fitzpatrick was not off the mark when she said she knew quite a few naval officers, immediately recognizing the guest of honor.

He was a handsome young man in his early thirties, playing the piano forte. A pretty lady wearing a charming blue silk gown with a necklace of milk-white pearls, which Kathleen could not help but admire, was standing cozily by his side turning the pages of music.

"Good heavens, if it isn't Commander Robert Smythe and our own wise woman, Sarah Duncan!" exclaimed Lady Agnes, upon entering the room.

She hurried up to the handsome couple.

Standing, the dark-haired naval officer and the young woman of almost angelic appearance, greeted

Lady Fitzpatrick and their newly arrived guests. The young woman, Kathleen was later informed, had a noted reputation as a wise woman. She was trained in the arts of healing and midwifery, and was much sought after by the chronically ill.

"Lady Fitzpatrick, this is indeed a most unexpected pleasure," said the officer, bowing over her hand.

"I knew Master Powers's guests were from Urlingford and that a sea captain's widow was among his party acting as companion for his ward, Lady Langtry, but this is indeed a most delightful surprise to have you here among us as one of our guests."

"And to be sure, the same can be said for me, *Captain*," beamed the widow.

She said his title, Kathleen noticed, with a small amount of added emphasis. Beau had informed them that their host had recently been promoted from a first lieutenant and acting master commander, to that of a captain of full rank. It was for this reason they were dining together. It was a small celebration of the momentous event.

"So you've been told," he said modestly. "Master Powers acted as my legal advisor to help clear my name before the Admiralty's Board of Inquiries. After all that nasty business that took place aboard The Brunswick, there was quite a bit of tidying up that needed to be done. My good commander, Captain Jackson, whom you will meet presently, aided him in giving testimony on my behalf."

"But did you know of his other most recent change in status, Lady Fitzpatrick?" asked Wise Sarah, the angelic beauty standing proudly by his side.

Lady Agnes shook her head. "No, do tell."

Although the knowing smile on her wrinkled face gave away the fact that she suspected something special had occurred between the wise woman and the young commander, she remained silent. It was evident she wanted the young woman to have the pleasure of telling them herself.

"He is no longer to be on the ship's lists as a bachelor. Show her, Robert," urged the young woman.

Grinning, Captain Smythe lifted up his left hand for inspection. On it he wore a plain wedding band. He placed an affectionate arm around his lovely bride and gave her a kiss on the cheek.

"Captain Jackson married us on my mother's island," Sarah explained, beaming with pride at her husband.

"And it was a service I was delighted to do," said a middle-aged officer of thin build joining them. The slightly yellow tinge of his skin informed them that he had recently been ill.

It had been reported in the local papers that Captain Jackson had been maliciously poisoned by a member of his own crew, creating quite a scandal. For no one expected such a villainous act to occur upon one of his majesty's naval vessels, and most certainly not against this stern, but fair-minded, officer.

Espying the ladies with the magistrate, Captain Jackson bowed to her and Lady Agnes.

"I see Master Powers brought with him two lovely creatures to grace the table. I am fair certain all the food will taste like ambrosia tonight for I shall be dining among goddesses."

Tittering, Lady Fitzpatrick lightly tapped his shoulder with her fan.

"*Musha*—such pretty words! I am after thinking, Captain Jackson, you have recently kissed the Blarney stone. For sure, I've never heard such flattery from a gentleman. Aye, sir, you meant two goddesses," she indicated Sarah and Kathleen. "And one old Methuselah, didn't you? At my age it would be foolish to expect you to put me in the exalted Venus category."

"Not at all, ma'am. I am certain the good captain meant what he said," put in Beau gallantly. "For does not the book of Proverbs say, as a man thinks in his heart, so he is. It is quite obvious to those of us who know you, Lady Fitzpatrick, you are not older than one and twenty at heart or in appearance. One can plainly see you are as winsome as any young lady still in her debutante whites."

Pleased, Lady Agnes smiled. "I am surrounded by blind flatterers, but faith, what can I do, ladies? They are such splendid gentlemen. And I've often been told never to argue with a man who buys ink by the barrel, as most assuredly you do, Master Powers."

Those around Lady Fitzgerald laughed, knowing she was referring to his professions both as a solicitor and magistrate. This happy merriment continued until a bell indicated that dinner was to be served. The only guests they had not yet met were introduced at the table.

"May I present First Lieutenant Litton; we served together under Captain Jackson aboard The Brunswick," said Captain Smythe, introducing them to an amiable, cherubic faced gentleman in his late twenties.

He stood and bowed to them.

"And this is his sister, Miss Emily Litton," he said, indicating the young lady seated across from him with mousy brown hair and spectacles.

She wore a tartan styled evening gown of green with black ribbons and red garnet jewelry. Despite her prim appearance, Kathleen was soon to learn Miss. Litton was a spirited young woman. The spinster kept them in stitches throughout the evening regaling them with tales about her past adventures as a rich widow's traveling companion.

The young lady explained, "Mrs. James Hamilton was from America. A place called Trenton, New Jersey. She hired me because I was English. She said she thought I would be able to order the Irish porters around better than her because of it."

At this remark, Lady Fitzpatrick interrupted with a loud harrumph.

"Shall I continue?" asked Miss. Hamilton, sensing the Irish lady's antagonism towards her late employer.

"Please . . ." said Lady Fitzpatrick stiffly with an indifferent wave of her hand.

"She was very eccentric, Mrs. Hamilton. She consulted a spiritualist in New York before hiring me. He told her I would not try and make-off with her jewels and other valuables—and suggested to her she should hire me. The lady, after checking her astrologist, then hired me on a day considered lucky. It was really quite grand traveling with Mrs. Hamilton. We stayed in some of the loveliest homes and hotels. But she was very superstitious. I cannot count the number of times we almost did not take a coach because she thought the day would bring misfortune. It was a wonder we traveled about as much as we did."

At that moment the cook arrived, a woman whose thin stick figure belied her ability to create delicious fare. She personally set the first course of beef soup, still steaming hot in a large Wedgwood tureen, on the table. The gentlemen helped serve the ladies.

Candelabras with branching arms lit the dining room. A large display of fruits, nuts, and grapes decorated the table's center in tiered serving platters.

The courses were served simply with Sheffield plates. They were made of silver and copper melded together. A Wedgwood porcelain dinner service with scenes of Greek temples and flowers in green and white were their plate settings. The utensils had matching ivory green-stained handles.

"These were gifts from Robert's crew," Sarah said, indicating the crystal wine and glass decanter etched with the Royal Navy's coat of arms. "They were specially ordered from Waterford."

"Well then, we must toast the Royal Navy and your husband's new rank with them," said Beau merrily as he poured the wine.

"Ladies and gentlemen," he said standing, gently knocking his fork against his glass, summoning their attention. "I wish to toast to the great success of my friend who recently showed unprecedented courage, and has now become newly appointed to the rank of captain. Please raise your glasses to Captain Robert Smythe of his Majesty's Royal Navy. Huzzah!"

At which point several other huzzahs were added by the guests. Beau raised his hand asking for a moment more. He said, "And to his lovely new bride, Mrs. Sarah Smythe, who has provided us with such delightful company and food."

"Hear, hear," was heard by everyone as all took a moment to sip from their wine glasses.

The toast was followed by a short prayer said by Captain Jackson, blessing the food and giving thanks for Robert's recent promotion. As was the custom, the guests helped each other choose from the dishes nearest them. This occasioned great gallantry among the gentlemen as they would not let the ladies lift the heavy platters.

"My dear," said Beau, frowning as Kathleen reached for the soup tureen containing beef broth. "Please let me assist you. Your small wrists, although lovely to view, should not have to lift such a heavy ladle."

He poured the soup out for the ladies nearest him and made excuses throughout the evening. Not once did they touch a ladle or serving fork.

He insisted, "You are such a delicate flower of femininity, Lady Langtry. You should not be forced to do any manual labor other than to be witty and charming for the rest of us to enjoy."

At this Miss Litton gave a small laugh, for he had said

a similar flattering remark to her. Whereupon Captain Jackson engaged the spinster with a question about one of her coach travels with the eccentric American.

"I see, sir." Kathleen smiled at Beau, knowing that he and the other gentlemen were competing to see who could be the most gallant. "That if I were to drop my handkerchief this moment into the gravy, you would jump in and rescue it with all the chivalry of a knight errant bent on winning a fair maiden's hand."

"Ah, that perhaps is true," agreed the Corinthian, turning his back on the rest of the company, screening his actions from view. He captured her hand where it lay lightly on her wine goblet.

"But it would not be solely the hand which I would be seeking, dear lady." With that he boldly lifted it.

His eyes remained fixed on her face. He brought it to his mouth to lightly kiss the inside of her wrist. The same one she'd dabbed perfume on when they were in the village shop. "I'm glad you continue to wear my favorite scent. Whenever I'm around roses or jasmine, they remind me of you."

Mesmerized, she could think of no reply. She felt as if his lips were branding her skin. Her blood swirled and her heart pounded with anticipation.

She almost chocked out her words, "I . . . am glad you are so pleased."

Glancing around the table, she wondered if the others had noticed what had passed between them. Secretly she was relieved they had not. The moment was too intimate to be shared.

The rest of the guests appeared to be occupied listening to a lively tale Miss Litton was engaged in recounting. It concerned an overturned traveling coach and a handsome Calvary officer who had come to their aid.

"I never was so surprised when upon arrival in Brighton who should pass us on horseback, but our rescuer!" exclaimed the spinster, ending her story.

The evening proceeded with several more courses of fish, turkey with chestnuts, purled carrots and onions, fried potatoes, and meat pies. The side dishes were fewer than what normally were served at Dovehill Hall, Kathleen noted. But this was to be expected. The guests were not numerous and the household was a modest naval one.

She found herself enjoying the evening immensely. It had been a long time since she'd spent time in the company of anyone younger than fifty. Her late husband had frequently entertained. But most of their guests had been gouty old men.

She'd detested every forced minute. The language of her late husband's cronies had been rough and crude. The conversations at the table had been rife with sexual innuendos and frequently the men unashamedly leered at the exposed portions of her skin.

Bangford had reveled in it. He made certain she wore low cut bodices to encourage them and would rebuke her when she dared to protest. "Not a word, Madame. You do as I say. I am your husband. I want my friends to see all of your lovely assets. I want their faces to turn pea-green with envy."

And thus forced to obey, she would comply. She had no other choice. As his wife he could have her beaten if she didn't. And he frequently reminded her of this.

The side dishes and tablecloth were removed. The last course, dessert, was served. A ginger pudding was set on the table with accompanying warmed custard and orange sauces.

As she took a bite, Kathleen was reminded that the late King George I, who'd come from Hanover, Germany, was known as "the pudding king," because he enjoyed the dessert. It was served to him during his first Christmas in Great Britain, making it thereafter a national tradition.

She could not fault the late king for liking it. She'd never tasted anything so delicious. Mrs. O'Grady had never allowed her to partake in sweets.

She was sternly told, "It will make you fat—and we mustn't allow that. You must keep your slim figure, your ladyship, in order to fit the gowns that Lord Langtry expects you to wear." And so it was that her husband and his dinner companions would indulge in the most decadent desserts, while Kathleen was only permitted a piece of fruit and a wedge of cheese. Now, for the first time in years, she let the citrus-flavored sauce and matching sweet bread roll over her tongue and lie on her taste buds. Unknowingly, she closed her eyes, savoring her first morsel. Daintily, she licked the spoon, enjoying each tangy bite.

She looked up and stared directly into Beau's eyes. He'd been intently watching her. There was, she could not mistake, a hungry look in his. He stared at her mouth as if he wished to taste her. And she realized she wanted him to kiss her again, like he had that evening in front of the fire. And she also realized something else. She wanted to kiss him back. Not in reaction to his kiss, but in a bold, sensual statement of her own. The spark that passed between them was interrupted by the laughter at the other end of the table where Miss Litton had been regaling the group with another witty story.

Along with the wobbly sweet pudding and fruit, two different types of bramble wines were served. After dessert the newly named captain's wife, Sarah Smythe, rose from the table, indicating it was time to leave the gentlemen to their port and cigars.

The ladies went back into the drawing-room for coffee, chocolate, and spice cake. They passed the time in genial conversation and a few hands of cards, until the men joined them.

Some music was called for, and obligingly, their

host, Captain Smythe, again played the piano forte. They sang together *Come Loose Every Sail to the Breeze* a tune well-known among the men in their company for it was often sung at sea.

Captain Jackson led them through the first part, singing in a fine contralto voice,

> *"Come loose every sail to the breeze.*
> *The course of my vessel improve.*
> *I've done with toils of the seas . . ."*

At which point he signaled to the rest of them to join in the chorus of

> *"Ye sailors, I'm done bound to my love.*
> *Ye sailors, I'm done bound to my love.*
> *I've done with toils of the seas.*
> *Ye sailors, I'm bound to my love . . ."*

With delighted laughter they finished. They gave applause in appreciation for Captain Smythe's fine piano playing, or as Beau commented, "For gamely keeping up with us squawking wobblers."

They paused, waiting to see who would lead the next song.

Beau boldly stepped forward. "I recently learned an Irish ballad called, *Down by Black Waterside*. I don't suppose you ladies know it?" he asked Lady Fitzpatrick and Mrs. Smythe, knowing they were both Irish.

"That is a delightful song," noted Lady Fitzpatrick. Mrs. Smythe readily concurred that it was a ditty worth hearing.

"Do sing it for us, Beau," urged Robert from the piano.

"Very well, but I must warn you, I refuse to be held accountable for any ladies swooning," he said rather immodestly to the delight of the rest of the guests.

"Indeed, sir, I shall try my best not to," Miss Litton replied gaily.

But the warning, thought Kathleen, should have been directed at her. It was she who almost swooned.

Her heart felt as if it would almost hammer out of her chest as he sang out in his fine baritone,

> *"Nine times I kissed her ruby lips*
> *I viewed her sparkling eye*
> *I took her by the lily-white hand,*
> *my lovely bride to be . . ."*

As he sang out the last chorus, she could not help but think of how he had held her hand and kissed it but a few minutes before.

When he finished, he looked directly at her and gave a small bow to the rest of his audience.

Lieutenant Litton came up and clapped him on the back, declaring, "*Demme*, but you are a fine singer, sir!"

"Would you like to take to the stage, Master Powers?" asked Miss Litton.

"Many thanks for your kind compliment, but alas, I am no Sheridan," he said, mentioning the famous Irish actor and writer. The Irishman currently ran Drury Lane Theater in London and was noted to be a fine singer.

"I prefer to save my pacing of the boards for the courtroom. There I am assured no one will throw rotten turnips at me," he said with a grin. He then directed his attention to Kathleen. "Lady Langtry, how did you find my singing?"

"Very fine, sir," she smiled, "very fine indeed . . ."

She could not help but clasp her hands together. A little nervous, she tried to hide them in the folds of her gown. She did not want him to think she connected the song with what had occurred between them earlier.

But correctly he interpreted her gesture.

"Merci," he said in French and deliberately took one of her hands to bow over.

This brought a blush to her cheeks. He was undoubtedly one of the most gallant gentlemen she had ever met. The attention he paid her was more than flattering. It was head spinning.

The evening ended pleasantly. When they returned to the townhouse, she realized she'd never enjoyed herself so much. Beau had invited her to meet his friends and she'd been at ease in their lively company. In fact, for the first time in a very long time she'd felt as though she belonged, a feeling that brought her both comfort and joy. She did not feel as if anyone was trying to find fault with her. Beau's friends had openly made it known they liked her.

She had been invited by the newly married captain's wife, Sarah, to join her on another day for tea. As a result, she now felt a warm feeling of happiness.

If her late husband had been alive, there would have been a post party review of her comportment. Mrs. O'Grady would have taken out her little black notebook and dissected every real or imagined fault she'd made. She would have then gone to bed demeaned and exhausted. But none of that had occurred. She'd been warmly welcomed and accepted by the entire party.

After they arrived back at the townhouse, Beau complimented them once again. "Thank you, for making this one of the most memorable evenings I've had the pleasure these past few weeks to enjoy."

He'd said he wanted to be worthy of her trust and become her friend. Tonight, he'd shown himself to be a true gentleman, intelligent, humorous, and respectful. And he'd exhibited a characteristic no gentleman of her close acquaintance ever had before . . . kindness. She was most fortunate to have him as her guardian and friend.

Yes, she decided, looking dreamily at the hand he'd kissed. Her life was different now, in so many ways—but she wondered a little sadly, how long would this happiness last? Would she be forced eventually to submit to someone else's whims? Or worse, possibly come to physical harm?

She thought of the gunman and how close she'd come to death. She shivered at the memory, knowing it hadn't been a mere coincidence.

The man who'd tried to shoot her wasn't a madman. It had been carefully planned. He'd been hiding among the trees waiting for her, and her alone. Of this she was almost certain. But why had he wanted to harm her? Was it because he personally knew her and held a grudge? If so, who was he? And what had she done to offend him?

She frowned in thought. She could think of no one who detested her. Most men had been too bedazzled by her husband's wealth and position to take offense when she refused their unwelcome advances.

And as for women, one dour face did enter her thoughts, Mrs. O'Grady. But she dismissed that possibility. The disgruntled housekeeper had retired to her deeded farm weeks ago and not been heard or seen from since.

But if it was not her, could it be someone had been hired to kill her, as Lady Fitzpatrick suggested? Possibly paid by one of her family members, as Robert believed?

This last thought disturbed her. She knew her dead husband's family and her uncle, Squire Lynch all too well. They were all coldhearted and money hungry enough to do it.

Secretly, despite her outer calm, she feared a repetition of what had occurred on the green. She silently prayed if she faced danger again, she would be strong enough to fight for her life and survive.

Chapter 6

They left Dublin the following week. The wedding of Lady Fitzpatrick's niece, Lady Beatrice O'Brien to Captain James Huntington, the new Earl of Drennan, was approaching. Lady Agnes was on tenterhooks in her eagerness to return to Urlingford. She wanted to ensure her niece was wed to the dashing earl in the grandest manner.

No repeat of the gunman incident had occurred since that foggy day on Saint Stephen's Green. The precautions were lifted, and Kathleen once again experienced the freedom of being able to take her rambling, solitary walks.

Tim, no longer tied to a leash, thrived in the countryside. He exuberantly ran across the green hills. In no time he doubled in both weight and size, removing any remaining fears she held concerning his health.

The wedding day of Lady Beatrice O'Brien to the Earl of Drennan was everything one could hope for. The sun hung like a bright yellow rose in the clear blue sky, and although it was early spring, a thin layer of white frost covered the ground.

The Drennan Chapel's pews were filled to capacity. The aristocrats were seated in a segregated part of the church nearest the altar. Many of the castle's tenant farmers stood in back, observing the sacred rite between their master and his soon to be new wife.

The paths leading to the chapel were decorated by the villagers with arching branches of evergreen and wildflowers. Inside the sanctuary itself green ivy tendrils decorated the end of the pews and the altar. Bouquets of Burnet Rose, a wild white rose that grew in abundance nearby, festooned the green centers.

Bagpipes echoed across the nearby hills as Lord Patrick O'Brien, the father of the bride, greeted the invited at the door with, "Peace be with ye . . . come in friend . . . aye, 'tis a grand day for a wedding. The very rich, as well as the poorest of the poor, attended. Peasants who lived in roadside mud and straw huts known as *scalpeens*, stood humbly outside. These impoverished peasants hoped to catch coins the newlyweds would toss after the service for good-luck. Later they would be invited to eat at the long trestle tables set outside. It did not carry any weight with Lord Patrick how rich or poor they were. He intended to share the joyous event of the marriage of his only child with the entire village.

Upon seeing the beautiful bride walk up the stone steps of the chapel, men took off their hats in respect, and ladies curtsied. The bride was about to become the new mistress of Drennan Castle. She was a powerful landed lady, one of the few remaining Irish gentry. They owed their living and the well-being of their families to her and the Earl of Drennan. Their good fortune was the villagers', as well.

Lady Beatrice O'Brien's wedding gown rivaled Princess Caroline of Brunswick's in embroidery, but instead of silver over silk, the Irish bride wore white lace over the rich fabric. The wedding gown had been crocheted by cloistered nuns from the local convent.

The bodice was embroidered with seed pearls. The flowing cathedral train depicted the heraldic emblems of the two families being joined. The rose and the shamrock were entwined together, delicately stitched in silk thread.

The bride's long black hair was swept up into a braided crown, delicately curled tendrils hung down from each side of her lovely oval face. The veil, which covered her hair, was held in place by a family heirloom, a tiara made of silver flowers and leaves, embedded with large pearls.

"Her gown was not finished until a few minutes ago," whispered a young farmer's wife standing nearby. "I saw her aunt, Lady Fitzpatrick, sew the last stitches of the hem herself, wanted to make certain they were in place before her niece entered the chapel to ensure the marriage was a lucky one."

Taking her father's arm, the bride, the lady once known despairingly as the Spinster of Brightwood Manor, stepped inside the chapel.

The congregation stood.

It was with a mixture of happiness and a touch of sadness, Kathleen watched her walk down the aisle. Kathleen had recently helped Lady Beatrice escape a forced marriage to a dastardly villain, who'd kidnapped Lady Beatrice in order to get his hands on her money. But she had not been able to help herself, years ago, being too young and unknowing of the world, to do the same.

She could not help but think of how different her own wedding might have been. If her parents had not died by typhoid fever, she might have married a man of her own age and choosing—someone who would have loved, honored, and respected her. Instead, she had been manipulated by her uncaring uncle into being leg-shackled to a controlling, old man.

Aye, she sighed, as the bride walked by, *my life would have been a very different one. I would have had the freedom to choose my own path. Possibly, I would not have felt so alone and unloved.*

She looked towards the altar where the groom, the dark and handsome Earl of Drennan, stood wearing his dress uniform as a captain in his Majesty's Army. The scar on his left cheek wrinkled as he smiled.

He wore a long sword that hung down by his side, a

weapon he was very familiar with. Handsome though the groom was, the man who held her attention was the light-haired Corinthian standing by his side. Acting as the earl's best man, Beau Powers was, as always, impeccably dressed, in a double breasted morning coat.

She wondered as she looked over at the handsome magistrate . . . *perhaps I will now be able to find a husband with whom I can share companionship, as well as love?* She remembered all the small kindnesses and protection he had provided her. In her reticule she carried the fan he had given her as an unexpected present.

Maybe not all men were like her late husband and Uncle Lynch? Perhaps there were men in the world who were different. Men, like her guardian, who were honorable and trustworthy. A man she might count upon in times of trouble.

Beau's eyes met hers as the young couple placed rings on each other's fingers. She was not aware of it, but hers had become a warm shade of light blue. For a moment she lost herself in his gaze, conscious only of him.

The spell was broken when the newly married couple turned to the priest for the final blessing. They gave each other their first kiss as husband and wife. It was sweet and touching. The love and joy on the young spouses' faces made everyone wish them a continued happy life.

A small figure dressed in brown silk leaned into Lord Patrick for support. He patted her hand. The bride's father and aunt had been openly weeping tears of joy during the short service. Their shared dream of seeing Lady Beatrice happily married to a titled gentleman had come true.

Aye, Kathleen decided, witnessing the scene, *I have merely to open my heart to the possibility that such a gentleman might exist and wish to be part of my life.* She was almost afraid to think the next thought. *Perhaps he would love and cherish me? Not for my face, nor for my wealth, but just for me . . . Kathleen.*

The priest at the altar inclined his head.

A small lad pulled on a long rope, ringing the chapel bells in celebration of the momentous event. She watched as the happy couple walked out of the sanctuary.

As Beau passed her pew, he gave her a saucy wink. She smiled back at him, delighted by the acknowledging gesture.

The reception was held outside under striped tents. The long trestle tables were set beneath as a precaution to keep them dry in the event that the few gray clouds hanging low overhead decided to pour rain on the festivities. The tables were filled with a variety of local dishes of cooked lamb, colcannon (a mixture of whipped potatoes and cabbage), fish, garden vegetables, meat pies, and soda bread. The entire village had been invited to partake in the festivities. No one was to go away hungry.

Gifts given to the couple were displayed on a separate table. The one that impressed many, and caused some envy among the gentlemen present, was the gift given by the bride's father, Lord Patrick. He had ensured himself that when the couple returned from their honeymoon in Italy, known in Irish as *mi na meala* (month of honey), their house would not be empty of strong brew.

He gave them enough mead (honey wine) to last through the first month of marriage and longer, although it was said the tea-drinking aunt had tried to talk the gentleman out of the gift and serving the brew at the reception.

"But, Agnes," the father said in his defense, "'Tis tradition . . . I'll not have anyone say m'daughter left my home empty-handed like a wandering pauper."

"As if anyone would be saying that, Paddy," replied the sister with a sniff. "For all and sundry know she is your only heir. She's been running your estates for years now, and you've been helping pay for that decrepit pile of bricks of theirs to be fixed into something resembling a proper castle. Nay, it was a sorry excuse t'use that still of yours to make some of the devil's brew. Aye, and don't be telling me different. Especially after ye solemnly promised me you wouldn't make any, after she walked down the aisle. I'm disappointed, Paddy."

"But, Agnes," protested the brother. "I did it for Bea'. It was for her I made the honey mead—not for myself."

"And the spirits I see being served? Where did they come from? I suppose the wee folk left those barrels overnight?" she asked, indignant.

She indicated the young newlyweds, who sat at the head table pouring spirits into silver toasting goblets, unaware of the argument taking place. The couple sipped from each other's glass, happily celebrating their union as man and wife.

Kathleen, who sat nearby listening to the conversation, noticed the stern lady's face soften. The tea-totaling sister was weakening. She sensed Lady Fitzpatrick would do anything to ensure her niece's present happiness, even bend some of her usual stubborn iron will.

The gentlemen guests, who had been gamely drinking lemonade, listened intently to the conversation. She could tell by the nodding of heads, they silently agreed with Lord Patrick. An Irish wedding without strong poteen (spirits distilled from potatoes) was deflating, and the entire parish knew his lordship's brew was the best.

"Very well, Paddy." The sister sighed.

The next remark she spoke was aimed at those standing nearby. "But there better not be any bodies lying about on the ground for my Beatrice to trip over in the morning—or by thunder, I'll come after them who drink too much and bring down my own bad luck upon their sodden heads."

"Nay—nay, there won't be," quickly reassured Lord Patrick, visibly brightening.

He bent over and kissed his sister warmly on the cheek. "You're a grand one, ye are, Agnes—the best of all sisters."

Smiling, Lady Fitzpatrick, shooed him away.

"Ye best be off and see to opening some of those barrels ye hid by the wedding cake. By the sour apple faces our gentlemen guests are wearing, one would think we were serving them ditchwater instead of lemonade."

After the toasts and speeches, a sudden commotion was heard. A group of oddly dressed men entered the clearing, waving their arms up and down, dancing with bells, and playing music on drums, pipes, and fiddle. They were dressed in women's clothing and wore pointy masks made of twisted straw to disguise their faces.

"The straw boys have come," said one of the village women across from her, laughing as one of them made a saucy gesture in her direction. "Aye for sure now, I recognize one of them. That's my eldest, Jeremy, wearing his sister's old petticoat and my moth eaten nightshirt."

"And there's Brian." The lady seated next to her noticed. "Musha, musha, I hope his father doesn't see him. He was supposed to stay home and tend the fire as punishment for missing mass yesterday. Not take part in any tomfoolery today."

One of the straw boys dressed like an old man went up to the bride and began to dance with her. Another, disguised as an old woman, twirled around the groom to bring the couple good luck and a happy long life.

The straw boys began taking guests by the hand as a fiddler gaily played. An unusually tall straw boy stood before her. He bowed and silently held out a hand, indicating he wanted her to dance with him.

She placed her hand wordlessly in his. He led her to the others and twirled her into his arms. She lightly placed a hand on his shoulder. His muscles felt strong and firm beneath her fingertips as they whirled in a tight circle. She looked into the straw boy's mask and his intelligent blue eyes met hers. She knew him—and it thrilled her.

They joined a group of revelers and linked with the other dancers into a large circle. They danced together, separated, and rejoined. Quickly, the straw boy spun her around and around. The music's tempo quickened until she began to laugh, giddy with delight.

"Please," she said, waving her hand in the air like a fan. "I need to catch my breath. I'm afraid I shall fall down. My head is spinning."

Solicitously, he stopped.

He led her to a bench underneath the courtyard's lone tree. They sat together, resting quietly, enjoying each other's company as they observed the others who continued to dance.

"This is beginning to itch," he said, lifting the mask a little to scratch.

Looking around, she noticed that several of the other straw boys had already removed theirs. "I think it's safe for you to take it off . . . Beau."

"Ah, much better," he remarked, setting it aside.

His blue eyes twinkled down at her. He ran a hand through his blond curls. Bits of straw fell, but a stray piece remained.

She lifted her hand and gently removed it.

The fiddler played a slow waltz. Couples danced boxed steps, smiling at the bride and groom who stood in the center. Enviously, she looked over at the newlyweds. They appeared to be very much in love.

"May I have the pleasure?" Beau asked, holding his hand out to her.

Giving a slight bow of the head, she stood.

Together they slowly danced under the wide spread branches of the old oak tree. The feel of their two bodies touching caused her to glow inside. Every part of her tingled, aware of his firm touch.

What would it be like if he kissed her right now, with his arms wrapped around her? Would all of her senses come alive? She looked up at him. She noted the line of his lips as they curved into a smile, the sharp roundness of his masculine chin, the way his deep blue eyes sparkled like a bright light bouncing off a dark river when they looked into her own. Aye, she suspected it would be quite unforgettable.

It was as the last notes of the waltz faded that the dark clouds above, which had been threatening all morning, finally rumbled. Light drops of rain fell. Guests quickly grabbed food and other items, hurriedly seeking shelter under the tarps and the castle's large keep.

But she stood with Beau silently, waltzing a few more steps—uncaring of the rain—dancing to their own rhythm of their beating hearts.

He bent his head and gently brushed his lips against hers.

Her heart thudded heavily as his arms tightened around her waist. She willingly leaned into him, fitting her body against his. The warmth she'd first felt caught flame. It coursed through her body as their mouths joined.

"Now ain't that a pretty sight," a sneering voice said thickly, nearby.

Turning her head, she noticed a pale, choleric looking man observing them. He was slouched drunkenly over one of the trestle tables, wearing an eyesore of a bright yellow morning coat. His clothes were in soiled disarray.

Much to her dismay she recognized her uncle, Squire Lynch. She had not seen him since the reading of the will.

"I heard tell you had a bit o' trouble in Dublin, Kathleen," he continued. "They say a man tried to sh-shoot you and a wretched monster of a dog saved your hide. What a damn shame . . . as one of your remaining relatives, I would have happily taken your place at Dovehill Hall."

Lifting a tankard of ale, he drained the contents. Some of it dribbled down his pointy chin. Pounding the center of his chest with the side of his fist, he loudly belched.

"K-kept her for your own, Powers?" he commented. "You wanted the blunt for your own pocket. I daresay— so I, nor anyone else, could have any." He smiled his yellow teeth at her in a leer. "Now you're his light-skirt, are ye, m'dear. First you were Langtry's, now you are this common tradesman's—"

"The devil you say," Beau said, his eyes narrowing. His right hand clenched into a fist. He took a step forward, as if he'd like to give the other man a good right hook to the jaw. But he hesitated and looked over at her. Her face showed a mixture of fright and worry. She had not expected this ugly confrontation on what should have been a happy occasion.

The rain was beginning to pour heavily down. He took off his coat and put it around her shoulders. "You had best go inside. We don't want you to catch a chill. I have something I need to discuss with your uncle before I join you."

Reluctantly, she turned and headed towards the keep. She did not know what was about to happen, but she sensed his anger towards her uncle. It was palpable.

Retribution was not far away. It was obvious Uncle Lynch was once again deep in dun territory with gambling and tailor's debts. He undoubtedly had come to the wedding to ask for her help. But now it was too late.

His snide remarks had drained away the small amount of compassion she might have once felt. She was reminded that it was he who had leg-shackled her to old Lord Langtry. And it was he, as a result, who had condemned her to years of loneliness, and imprisonment.

Aye, let Beau deal with him, she decided grimly.

If he gives him a facer, I'll not be one to scold. I've had more than my belly full of my uncle. It was because of him my innocence was taken away. And I'll not be forgetting that anytime soon. Thus resolved, she went inside to join the other guests.

The remainder of the guests had already dried out and begun a sing along. The tune of *The Rose of Killarney* was belted out by the gentlemen gathered. The groom, having put his sword to good use, delicately fed whiskey soaked wedding cake to his lovely bride who sat happily on his knees.

A few minutes later, Beau joined Kathleen.

Wisely, she did not ask what had passed between the two men. She could tell from his grim expression, her uncle might be wearing a shiner around his eye the next time he dared to make an appearance.

But it was not to be. In the morning as two servants took down the sagging wet tents, a man was found lying on the ground. A straw boy's mask had been placed over his head, hiding his face.

"We best be getting him up and about before Lady Fitzpatrick sees him," said Tommy, one of Lord Patrick's servants. "She'll be after my master's hide if he's still here when her niece and the earl leave today."

"Aye, I wouldn't want to be the one to cause her ladyship to lose her temper," agreed the other, leaning over the man to shake him awake.

But the gentleman would not be roused. And turning him over they were soon to discover the cause . . .

The mask fell off.

A face with blue-tinged skin, and bulging eyes, greeted them. He was not breathing. He was as cold as ice. "Blessed Saint Christopher . . . it's Squire Lynch . . . and it looks as if he's dead." Tommy gasped, startled by the sight of the man's blue face.

"Look there . . ." The other pointed to the squire's coat. "A shot has gone straight through his heart."

"He's been murdered," Tommy said, stating the obvious. They turned frightened faces towards each other and ran to the castle.

Chapter 7

The village's constable and priest were quickly sent for. Prayers were said over the deceased's body and an inquiry was made concerning the murder. It was revealed by the servants that they had last seen Squire Lynch alive and holding his swollen left eye after Beau rejoined the party.

"Aye, I never thought a magistrate, and such a noted one from Tipperary at that, would do such a terrible thing and shoot his ward's uncle in a pique of anger. Nay, I never believed it," said the village constable upon hearing the servants' testimonies.

Kathleen tightened her mouth disapprovingly. She could not fathom why the constable had not made any proper apologies. He had upon his arrival confined Beau to a smoking room—for hours he was kept under lock and key like a common criminal. An armed guard was insultingly posted at the door. The earl and his new bride had tried to intercede, but to no avail. The law was the law.

All smiles, the constable released him.

"Aye, he's a gentleman of quality Master Powers is—killing another gentleman would never have done."

"Why I never," she said huffily. The audacity of the man!

She walked over and clasped Beau's hand in solidarity. She had protested at the unnecessary confinement from the very beginning, never believing for a moment he was to blame. To her thinking, the constable was an incompetent nincompoop!

Beau patted her hand and said, "Do not be angry at the constable, my dear. He was merely doing what I myself would have done."

"But only after the evidence was heard," she said, stiffly indignant.

"Kathleen," he said, dismissing the incident as a trifle. He was concerned about more pressing matters. "I do not know what is occurring here, but I fear for your safety. There are too many coincidences connected between the shooting in Dublin and your uncle's untimely death. For me not to think they somehow do not concern you as well would be foolhardy."

"But what about his gambling debts?" she suggested as a reason for the murder. "Maybe someone decided to kill him in order to collect on them? Perhaps they thought I would pay them off."

"I do not believe that is possible. If your uncle's life was in danger, he would have taken flight. Instead, he remained here in Urlingford in full view of everyone. And mind your uncle was not a strong-willed man. They could have easily shaken anything they wanted out of him. The gold buttons and the gemmed shoe buckles he wore last night were worth a small fortune."

She did not refute his argument. Her uncle had always managed to pay off his debts, keeping one step ahead of prison and any punishment that money-lending sharks might have devised for him. Admittedly, she too sensed that the two incidents might be connected. But she wanted to dismiss the evidence. She did not want her movements to be again curtailed. She was weary of imposed restraints. Her late husband had kept a close eye on her, restricting her movements to such an extent that she'd felt herself to be a prisoner. And now, she was again placed in a similar position, out of fear for her safety.

"Ah . . . the glum face again," he said, giving her a smile of understanding.

"What do you mean?"

"It's the way you look, my dear lady, when you are

unhappy." He touched the center of her forehead. "You crease a frown right here."

She touched the spot on her face.

"Do I? I never noticed."

"And I am afraid a party this time will not be the remedy," he said grimly.

"But what will?"

"Finding your uncle's killer and putting behind all the sad connections with your past. You have not exactly led what one would call a happy life."

"No, I haven't," she said with a small sigh in her voice.

She thought of her parents' deaths, her forced marriage to Langtry, the shooting in Dublin, and finally her uncle's murder. She doubted any other young lady of her age had experienced so many disturbing events in one short lifetime.

But standing next to her was a man who could help her forget the past, and she appreciated it. She squeezed his hand tighter to reassure herself he was real. He was not going to abandon her. He was not going to become like the other men who had entered her life and used her. No, he was standing solidly by her side.

He was right, she silently decided. She had best resign herself to once again being constantly watched. It was for her protection.

With certainty, she knew Beau would help her solve what appeared to be an insurmountable problem. They would find out together who had killed her uncle. Then, she would be free to embrace her new life unencumbered by the past.

*　*　*

One day later she stood at her uncle's graveside. Only a handful of villagers were in attendance. The squire had not been well-liked by anyone.

She did shed a few tears, remembering when he first took her in. After her parents' deaths, her uncle had been kind to her. She wanted to remember those early years. Before his warmth towards her, like the few good memories she had left, faded away.

Most of the mourners, she soon learned, had come to collect on past debts. As the squire's only living relative, she paid for the funeral. A dreadful mistake, she soon discovered. As soon as the purse strings were opened, every Jack-man tradesman who had a bill to settle came running.

Nefarious looking individuals within days quickly followed. These gamblers, carrying questionable markers, were placed in Beau's capable hands. And they were quickly dispatched with the same ease as one dealt with unwanted rubbish. A few sported boot prints on the backside of their breeches as they were flung out the side trade entrance door.

Her late husband's family, the Countess Deuville and her son, Henry, unexpectedly arrived at Dovehill Hall to offer their condolences. They were dressed in mourning black, reminding her of carrion crows.

"I suppose we are your only living relatives now, Kathleen," said the countess in a smug manner. The older woman eyed her up and down. "Widowhood suits you. You should never remarry, my dear, I am quite certain my brother would not have wished it."

"But I have every intention of doing so, Countess," she replied forthrightly, wanting to be contrary.

She didn't like being told what to do with her life. It was hers to do with as she wanted, without this interfering thorn in her side.

The older lady's eyes narrowed.

"If you do, I hope it is not to some man involved in trade," she said pointedly looking a Beau who stood by her side. "Have you written your will yet? I suppose you intend on leaving everything to your nephew, Henry. He is, after all, the sole remaining heir."

"I have not yet decided," she murmured, thinking how this might be the cause of her uncle's murder.

Aye, she decided, reminding herself of how her uncle had sold her to Langtry. When one becomes greedy enough, one is capable of doing almost anything, even hiring an assassin to commit murder.

Could one of her late husband's relations have killed her uncle? Maybe hired the assassin who shot at her in Dublin?

"It is an issue Lady Langtry is considering," explained Beau, solidly giving her his support. "This is not as straight forward as it may appear, Countess."

"There are various charities I am considering giving to," Kathleen said. "Master Powers is helping me write a will. We are considering having a trusteeship created."

"Indeed . . . and your companion, Lady Fitzpatrick, I do not see her here. What has become of that imposing lady?" the countess asked, changing the subject.

She eyed the handsome solicitor up and down with an insolent expression. "Surely you do not dwell here by yourself, my dear. That would be most unseemly. Perhaps it would be best if Henry and I stayed on and watched over you? You are far too young to be left here alone with a bachelor."

"Since the wedding of her niece, Lady Fitzpatrick has returned to her home in Urlingford. As for you and Henry remaining here to keep Lady Langtry company, I do not think that will be necessary. The new housekeeper and servants are more than adequate chaperones," replied Beau on her behalf, dismissing the fears as irrelevant.

Kathleen inwardly breathed a sigh of relief. She did not want her late husband's sister and lecherous nephew near her, let alone living with her. She knew Beau was informing the countess he would not tolerate any meddlesome interference.

The countess's mouth tightened. Her gray ghoul eyes sparkled dangerously in the dandy's direction. It was evident she was not used to being contradicted. She prepared to open her mouth to do verbal battle, but Kathleen interfered before she could speak.

"I agree with Master Powers. It is kind of you to offer, Countess. But we rub along quite well together, as you may have noticed, without anyone else's help. Indeed, I do believe it would be best if on the morrow you returned to London. No doubt there are more pressing matters at Saint James Court for you and Henry to attend to."

Or somebody else you can bother, she silently added.

Her blue eyes sparkled with determination. She was not going to submit to the countess or anyone else. She had decided never again to let that happen.

Her will from now on, she silently vowed, was going to be her own. With Beau's guidance, she would make her own decisions and live the way she wished. She finally had her freedom. She was not about to hand it over to another domineering tyrant.

After waving goodbye to the countess and Henry on the portico steps, she turned to Beau and said, "If I should suddenly drop dead, do me a great service, see to it they don't receive a farthing more than my uncle did."

His face hardened at the thought. He would kill anyone who would dare hurt her, including those two interfering aristocrats.

"I will protect you against anyone who would try to lay a hand against you," he vowed. "And see them sent to Hades itself."

She asked half-teasingly, "Am I that valuable to you, Beau? You would protect me against a greedy countess and her gnome-eyed son?"

"Yes—vixen, I would." He breathed, releasing the tension he felt.

He pulled her into his arms and kissed her with all the passion he felt. It didn't matter how important the person or how dangerous the situation, he would protect her. Even place his body in jeopardy.

She responded to his kiss, hesitantly at first, and then with growing confidence. He moaned and drew her closer. He knew he shouldn't, but he wanted her with every bone in his body. He was drawn to her, as he had never been with any other woman. She had a gentle nature, and yet she was unbreakably strong. She was sweet, and yet tart in her conversations with him. She was a tantalizing mix of ingénue and siren and he wanted to know her—deeply and completely.

Suddenly, she drew away from him. She gazed at him with a frown of worry. "Beau, I . . . I don't know how to make love."

Startled, he gave her a quizzical look, not fully understanding her discomfort.

Feeling heat rise to her face, she fingered the brooch, touching the love knot while confessing one of the secrets of her marriage to old Lord Langtry.

"What I mean is that I . . . I've never properly been made love to," she continued, letting the words rush out of her mouth, "not in the real sense that a wife normally experiences with a husband or lover."

"Are you saying you're a virgin?"

"No, not that . . . Bangford tried to make me *enceinte*," she said, embarrassed, using the French word for pregnant, uncomfortably remembering the village physician checking to be certain that she could bear children. Much to her relief, it had not been her inability, but Bangford's.

"My late husband lacked the stamina to . . . um, make me with child," she said hesitantly, "and when he made love to me, it was never with any tenderness or affection," she said with her eyes lowered. "I did not enjoy it. It was, to be truthful, most unpleasant."

"Kathleen," he said, taking her two hands into his, gazing into her wary blue eyes. "Until now our exchanges of affection, hugs, kisses, and so forth, have they been agreeable to you?"

"Yes," she answered honestly, remembering the pleasurable moments they'd shared together, how he'd made her toes curl with his intimate embraces.

"Kathleen, you are a gentle lady. A woman I respect and admire. I don't want to make you uncomfortable in any way. But from the first moment I met you, on that fateful day, I have wanted—"

"I want you, too," she said interrupting him, gazing into his eyes. "I am a woman with a mind of my own. For several years I was in a loveless marriage. Never experiencing the true wonder of what it could be like between a man and a woman," she said in her honest, straightforward way. "But I want to know that close intimacy now with you, Beau."

"Tonight, we will make love," he whispered into her ear, sending a delightful shiver throughout her body. "Have no fear. It'll be nothing like what you experienced before, of that I most solemnly swear."

Still uncertain, but with a glowing anticipation in her eyes, she silently nodded in agreement.

* * *

In the evening, as she brushed out her long golden hair, she felt her heart pounding in anticipation of Beau's arrival. Putting down the brush, she sprayed herself with jasmine perfume, remembering when he'd helped her buy her first bottle after her husband's death, how liberating an experience it had been. The simple act had brought her unexpected pleasure. Since then, she'd felt like a flower, unfolding, basking in the light of his kind attention. Nervously, she worried that their lovemaking might ruin their relationship and be a repeat of what she'd experienced with her late husband, that it would hurt, or worse, be demeaning . . . But then she thought about the warm kisses she'd shared with Beau, and was reassured. They had all been enjoyable.

She wondered, would their lovemaking be as wonderful as their kissing? Would his touch make her hot, tingly, leaving her breathlessly wanting to press herself up against him? She hoped so. She wanted to be close to him.

She stood and opened the large armoire in which she kept the expensive garments her late husband had bought for her. Inside a box, above the low-cut ball gowns and stunning frocks ordered from Paris, was a negligee of rose color with a matching silk robe, one she'd never before worn. She brought the box down, removing the negligee, sliding it down over her body.

Standing in front of a full-length mirror, she smiled at how sensual it made her feel. The silk clung smoothly to the curves of her body, emphasizing her full round breasts, the garment cupping them with wisps of silk and lace. She was happy her late husband had never seen her wear it; there were no unpleasant memories attached to the lovely gown to make her cringe.

As the clock on the fireplace mantel tolled the hour, a soft knock on the door alerted her to Beau's arrival.

She called out nervously, "*Entrez!*"

He entered, wearing a red-velvet smoking jacket and a paisley scarf wrapped around his neck. Shirtless underneath, golden chest hairs peeked through the neck of the jacket's dark lapels. She admired the broadness of his firm, muscular chest. The oriental styled silks he wore as trousers outlined his firm thighs.

They stared at each other for a moment as the pile of

logs burst into a crackling flame in the fireplace, releasing smoke and heat.

"You are exquisite," he said with wonder in his voice.

She sighed in relief, at his words. The way he was looking at her made her feel like the most desirable woman in the world. She liked that feeling. "What do we do next?" she asked, nervously biting down on her lower lip, her blues eyes locking with his.

"We love each other," he said, observing her.

"And how do we do that?"

"By touching each other . . . and you, my dear Kathleen, start first . . ."

"What do I do?" she asked, enjoying the fact that she would be in control.

"Whatever you wish," he answered, barely speaking above a whisper, his sapphire blue eyes gleaming with warm desire as he observed her movements.

Emboldened, realizing that she was the one who'd decide what they did, she drew closer to him. She stood in front of him, breathing in the clean smell of him, slowly removing the paisley scarf he wore around his neck. She let the fabric fall through her fingertips, dropping it to the floor.

"I want you to kiss me," she whispered into his ear.

"As you wish," he said, and lowering his head, pressed his lips up against hers as she brought her arms around his neck.

She explored his mouth with hers, their tongues entwining, her hips pressing up against his, a throb of desire beginning to pulse inside the lower region of her body. She could feel his manhood grow hard beneath the silk fabric. Stopping their kissing, she looked down at the bulge where his manhood was hidden.

"Can I touch it?" she asked breathlessly, her blue eyes shining with awakening desire and curiosity.

Silently, he nodded his head and taking her hand, he opened his loosened silk trousers and brought it down to his hardened manhood.

"Cup it here," he said, barely able to breathe, as she did as he asked.

"It's so smooth and warm . . . and yet so hard," she murmured, stroking it.

Her eyes widened at the unexpected feel of his skin beneath her fingertips. She boldly touched him, feeling the weight of the two round spheres hanging beneath the long shaft of hardened skin.

"I care a great deal about you, Kathleen," he said, his eyes softening, as he tenderly looked down at her, the golden strands of her hair gleaming in the firelight. "Are you certain you wish to continue with this?"

She nodded her head. "Yes, Beau . . . please make love to me."

"As you wish," he said. He picked her up, effortlessly carrying her to the large four-poster bed. She could feel his strong arms beneath her, and she felt secretly thrilled at his power . . .

He gently laid her down. Removing his clothing, he positioned himself next to her and pulling her into his arms began kissing her, nibbling on her lower lip, exploring, his mouth placing kisses along her neck and shoulder blades. The throbbing she'd felt earlier increased as he pulled down the bodice of her negligee, first cupping and then kissing her breasts, his tongue swirling around the hardened centers.

She gasped, arching her back upwards in response. Never had she felt such overwhelming sensations, as he tugged on her sensitive flesh with his teeth, making her moan.

She wanted to give him the same pleasure and wondered if she copied him, if it would have the same effect. He groaned as she trailed kisses down his neck and firm chest, pausing to suck on his nipples. His fingers began their own exploration down her body. She stopped her nuzzling when she felt his fingers enter her womanhood. He began stroking her core, gently inserting his fingers, feeling her moist heat.

"You are so wet for me, darling," he whispered in her ear.

"Is that good?" she replied, never having experienced these feelings before.

"It's very good." He smiled into the side of her neck. "It means your body is ready for me."

Emboldened, she reached up and pulled down his face to her, kissing him with all the passion she felt.

He responded, groaning, as he pressed his aching manhood against her. Without any hesitation, she boldly took his shaft in her hands, sliding it into her body's wet center. "Kathleen," he murmured, his eyes widening with surprise at her unexpected boldness. She grabbed hold of his buttocks, pulling him forcefully down onto her body, thrusting her pelvis upwards, until his body completely joined with hers.

"Ah . . ." he groaned with pleasure. "You feel like heaven."

"So do you," she replied breathlessly. She gasped with the pleasure of his movements, and began to meet his thrusts, awkwardly at first, and then with more daring and passion.

He lifted his hips and began to increase the tempo of their lovemaking, his manhood sliding up and down inside of her until she felt a delicious pressure build up inside of her. She had never felt it before. She kept meeting his thrusts, and then the feeling suddenly burst inside of her like a thousand shooting stars. Her eyes opened in wonder, and she almost lost her breath with the beauty of it.

She clung to him, floating on wave after wave of pleasure, flooding her entire being. It was an experience she'd never felt before. She cried out his name, letting the pulsing wave overtake her completely.

Beau rolled to one side. He breathed heavy, one hand holding his manhood while the other clenched the sheets. He then let out a soft shout and released his seed. His body relaxed again, and he turned towards her, gently kissing her on the lips.

"Are you all right?" he asked in concern, stroking her hair.

She nodded her head. "I'm fine, Beau. Our lovemaking, it was nothing like what I'd experienced before . . . it was wonderful."

"It was for me, too," he answered.

"It was?"

"Yes."

"Why do you doubt?"

"Because you're more experienced than I. And you've been with many women," she confessed, referring to his reputation.

"Kathleen," he said as he gathered her into his arms. "I may have had dalliances in the past, but I've never met anyone like you. You have qualities of character I respect. You're courageous, honest, and outspoken. I must confess, I'm very much attracted to you."

Her mouth opened in a round "O" of surprise. She had not expected him to make such a declaration.

He gently kissed her on the lips, and reassuringly he held her until she fell into a deep, contented sleep.

In the morning, when she awoke, Beau entered carrying her morning tray. He had placed a rose in a vase along with the food.

"Are you all right?" he asked, putting it down next to her on the bed.

She nodded, savoring the smell of the rose, eyeing him, the memories of their heated lovemaking forgotten as she felt a cold fear of impending entrapment,

"But not quite all right," he said, touching the center of her forehead where a frown now appeared.

"Beau," she said, confessing her concern, "You won't force me into marrying you, will you?"

"You don't wish to marry me?" he asked with a half-laugh.

Shamefacedly, she fingered the coverlet, unable to look him in the eyes, and answered, "It's just that I'm tired of being controlled. I like my freedom, Beau. Do you understand?"

He nodded. Taking her hand into his, he kissed it and said, "I will not ask you to marry me, unless you desire me to do so. For now, we will be very . . ." He kissed her on the lips. "Very, good friends . . ." He lowered the negligee's bodice, kissing her breasts.

"Oh." She breathed out, her blue eyes shining with reawakened desire. "Will we?"

Before he was tempted to completely undress her and make love again, he walked to the door and before parting, he smiled gently closing the door. Picking up the rose and smelling it, she almost wished he hadn't left.

Chapter 8

"There is something I wish to show you," Beau said quietly that evening as he entered the drawing room.

Mysteriously, he closed and locked the double doors behind him. He lifted his index finger up to his lips. "I don't want the servants to overhear what I have to say. It's a secret, very hush—hush . . ."

"Indeed," she exclaimed, lifting her eyebrows in surprise. She set aside the book of poetry she'd been reading.

He brought into the room an unfurled map of Dovehill Hall. The lake and off-shooting rivers, which flowed from it, were marked. Carefully, he spread the parchment out on the long study table next to her.

"What is this?" she asked.

"I found it among your late husband's papers, locked in a library adjoining his bedchamber. By the by, thank you for the loan of your keys," he said, handing them back. "I discovered several important documents concerning properties you own. And as I was sorting through them, I made this little discovery."

He indicated the map.

"It would appear," he paused before delivering the news, "to be a treasure map. It may possibly be the source of your husband's mysterious supply of rare antiquities and gems."

"The ones he would auction off?" she asked, interested.

He nodded his head.

"Is it really a treasure map?" She breathed. She stood to get a better view of the markings inked on the thin parchment. "What leads you to believe that?"

"This . . ." he said, gently removing the love knot

brooch from her shawl. He pointed to an identical design drawn on the map. "And this . . ." He laid a finger on what appeared to be a cave with a treasure chest drawn in the center. A drawing of valuable items surrounded and spilled out of the container. Above it a pirate's flag of a skull and bones flew.

"Pirates." She shuddered.

She remembered the conversation shared at Captain Smythe's table. The naval officers had recounted frightening tales about confrontations they'd had with marauding black marketeers and their ships. These lawless plunderers were notoriously ruthless. When provoked, they became bloodthirsty cutthroats.

"But how can this be?" she asked. "Bangford was an invalid. He never left the hall. So where did this treasure come from?"

"He may have been given the map when he bought the monastery, but it is difficult to tell. I am beginning to think that perhaps your brooch was used as a sign to mark entrances into the cave or other places of hiding, quite possibly both. During Cromwell's time, these secret hideaways may have hidden people, as well."

"Such as the monks?"

"Or valuables from raiders," added Beau, thinking of the much earlier occupants of the hill and lake, the Druids. "They would have had to face invaders . . . Vikings, Romans, and rival clans. Maybe these hiding places and their secrets were passed down to the different owners of the land upon occupation."

"But what of the treasure marked here?" she asked, pointing to the cave located off one of the rivers. "Do you think it's still there?"

"I do," he said and nodded his head. "We know it's real because of your brooch . . . As for the gems, Lord Langtry may have had connections with black-market pirates who obtained them for him. I believe he used the loot to pay for his expensive eccentricities. As for the pirates, they could be using the interconnecting canals and rivers that branch off from the lake, to come and go unnoticed by the law."

"Dovehill Hall . . . a haven for pirates." She gasped, astonished. How had her late husband become involved with such dangerous villains?

She tried to picture her invalid husband with a group of pirates. It was unthinkable. Bangford had always been so particular about the objects and people he surrounded himself with. To think of him associating with men of such low character defied what she had previously known about him, and yet there had been times, she reluctantly remembered, when his dinner guests had been less than genteel.

She recalled one evening when she had been told to make a brief appearance at the dinner table. It was one of the few times her husband had not wanted her to wear one of the exquisite silk evening gowns he'd had made for her. Instead she appeared in a modest, long-sleeved gown of stamped cotton.

The gentlemen present had spoken in loud voices and drunk large quantities of rum. The dark hooded looks they directed at her during dinner had made her nervous. It was as if they were ready to plunder her person right in front of her husband. She'd been happy to leave when it was time for the men to retire to the smoking room.

Now she understood why her nerves had been on edge. She had sensed the danger, knowing the unsaid— their guests were in reality pirates

"Maybe this treasure is why my uncle was killed? And the countess and Henry . . . do you think they know about it?"

"It's possible," he said, nodding his head, "they may have wanted to take control of Dovehill Hall and the treasure."

"What do you advise me to do?"

"I think a little exploring is called for, but I don't want to arouse suspicion. Perhaps I could take a trip to the treasure chest's hiding place."

"I'm coming with you," she said quickly, not considering the danger.

"No—I can't permit you," he replied, shaking his head in disagreement. "Your life has been put in danger already. And now with your uncle's death, I don't dare let you come with me. You would be too tempting a target."

"I'm coming," she repeated with more determination. "You need my brooch and where it goes, I go. The locals say the banshee gave it to me as a gift. I believe them. The spirit gave the brooch to me in order to find the treasure—I'm coming."

He lifted one of his hands in a gesture of protest.

She flinched in reaction.

His hands fell immediately to his side. He frowned. She had thought he was going to hit her. How was that possible? Had he not yet earned her trust? Did their lovemaking not make any difference? Were the ghosts of the men who had mistreated her forever to stand between them?

"You could be hurt," he said quietly. He gently took her hand. "I am only trying to protect you from harm. Please, understand, I would never do anything to hurt you."

She nodded her head and admitted, "I realize you're trying to protect me. I suppose it is because I've been so badly hurt in the past I am now behaving this way. It is true you have always been kind to me and last night was wonderful." She gave him a reassuring smile. "I'll be fine," she insisted bravely, refusing to be dissuaded. "I intend on going with you. The possibility of being hurt is a risk I am willing to take. Now, what excuse shall we give the servants?"

He nodded his head, silently considering . . . he was

going to have to give in to her desire to accompany him. It had been unbearable seeing her flinch away from him. He couldn't bear to think about what her life with her husband had been like, but he felt a strong urge to visit the dead lord's grave and spit on it.

"You and I will tell them we have decided to go on a picnic and plan to do a little boating. It will provide us with the perfect excuse to search for the treasure's cave and to show off my superb rowing skills," he said. Grinning, he flexed a muscle. "Mind, I haven't boated since I was a lad, but I think I can still handle a pair of rowing oars."

Understanding the charade they were about to play, she laughed.

"But you and I will be completely alone, without a chaperone, sir," she mocked, widening her blue eyes, pretending to be scandalized. "What will my sister-in-law think if one of the servants reports to her about our little excursion?"

"Undoubtedly the worst, but to be certain I think I had best practice making her nightmares a reality," he said, boldly placing a hand upon her waist.

His smile broadened and he gathered her into his arms.

He bent his head and their lips met as he gave her a passionate kiss, charged with the heady excitement of the upcoming adventure, worthy of a knight errant kissing his sweetheart before charging off on a valiant quest. A sizzling heat rushed through her. At that moment a whole horde of angry pirates could have entered the room and she would not have cared. It was as if they were both under an enchanted spell and nothing else mattered.

He took her hand and led her over to the striped, blue-and-white brocaded love sofa.

"Sir," said Kathleen, smiling, realizing they were

about to make love in the library. "Is this to be a part of my studies on lovemaking?"

"Indeed it is, my dear," he muttered, as he unsuccessfully tried to loosen her bodice front. "Blast . . ." A small tear was heard.

"Let me," she said, and with the skill of one who'd done it many times before, easily unlaced the garment. She then removed the morning gown and stepping out of it stood above him wearing only her corset, stockings, and garter. He removed his coat and shirt, his cuff links dropping unheedingly to the floor in his haste to undress.

"And the art of unbuttoning a gentleman's trouser, is that to be a part of my training?" she asked, coyly looking down to where a familiar bulge had made its appearance beneath his dark breeches.

"Indeed . . ." he said, sitting on the love sofa, observing her. "If you so wish it to be."

Without hesitation, she began unbuttoning the front flaps of the garment, and reaching inside, cupped his manhood as she had the night before. To her delight, it grew in her hands.

She eyed his manhood and asked, "May I sit on you?"

He lifted his blond eyebrows, surprised by the request.

"You realize that this is in the way . . ." He gestured down to his erect manhood.

"Exactly," she said and without any hesitation, she opened the slit of her undergarment and situated herself on top of him. His hands reached around and firmly held her buttocks in place, steadying her.

"Hmm . . . easier than learning to ride a horse," she said, placing her arms around his neck, comfortably situating herself on top of his manhood.

He laughed at her unusual comparison, but was not given the opportunity to comment on her riding abilities as she began kissing him, distracting him away from any thoughts he might have uttered.

She gently lifted her hips up and down, feeling the pleasurable increase of throbbing below as she slid along his hardened manhood, using the walls of her body's most secret of places to hold them together. She rode him, the throbbing increasing until she felt a powerful rush of light and energy burst through her body. She tensed, grabbing hold of his strong, muscular shoulders as he held her in place until the overwhelming waves of pleasure ceased.

Beau's face constricted. He lifted her from him. He tightened his abdomen, his breath heavy from the effort of not releasing his seed into her. His breathing slowly returned to normal, and gently he moved aside one of the long strands of her golden hair, which had fallen during their lovemaking.

"I think, Kathleen, you need no more lessons," he said, looking into her shining, bright, cornflower blue eyes. "You have graduated, and know enough now to plunder a man's body for your own pleasure."

"Indeed," she replied, smiling, happy that their lovemaking had been of mutual gratification. She felt powerful and it was because of him. He had helped her experience the true pleasure a man and a woman could enjoy if they cared about each other.

And, her heart silently added, loved each other . . .

She placed a quick kiss on his mouth, not willing to dwell on the fact that "love" was what she felt when she joined her body with his.

"Thank-you, dear professor, for your lessons . . . you were an excellent instructor."

"The pleasure, my lady, was all mine," he replied, kissing her back. "Now that you have plundered my body, perhaps you can help me find another type of treasure, as well?"

"Most willingly," she said, and thought of the secret treasure linked to the lover's knot and the pirates. Aye, an exciting adventure awaited them!

* * *

The blue of the sky shone off the sparkling water. Beau carefully helped her into the boat. He handed her a wicker basket full of food and a clay jug filled with lemonade.

He stepped in and once seated, picked up the oars. They had decided to float towards a remote portion of the south shore of the lake, drifting on a side river not far from the treasure's cave. She leaned back into the large cushions behind her. Lazily, she dipped her fingers in the water.

She watched him row, a dreamy smile on her lips, remembering their passionate lovemaking.

He had taken off his morning coat and the sleeves of his shirt were rolled up. In the sunlight the well-formed muscles of his arms gleamed. Even in this sweaty state, he looked, well, dashing.

From the lake she could see Dovehill Hall's Gothic form. It stood outlined against the backdrop of the sky. The towers and square main building dominated the hill's foreground.

Suddenly out of the corner of her eye she spotted a dark four-legged creature. It loped down the expansive green lawn. A black plumed tail wagged back and forth as it headed straight towards them.

"Tim," she said aloud.

She sat up on her elbows to get a better view of her pet. A broken rope dangled from the dog's neck. Evidently, he'd chewed through his leash.

"It looks as if the stable hands have lost track of him again," Beau commented, watching as the small black figure jumped into the water. "Shall we bring him aboard? Or do you want me to send him back?"

"We may as well have him join us," she said with a small sigh. "He will follow us regardless of what we decide. And I fear he might come to harm treading this deep water."

Once the dog reached them, Beau hauled him aboard.

Tim, realizing he was not going to be sent back, appreciatively licked his face. That done, he shook out his coat, spraying water all over them. Commanded to sit, the pet settled in the bow of the light skiff, taking on the job of watchdog. Noisily, he barked at the water fowl ahead, sending the birds into startled flight.

They reached a portion of the lake that curved in a serpentine manner. The land next to it was flat before it became overrun with dense shrubbery. Farther down was the side river, which they hoped would lead them to the hidden cave and its treasure. It interconnected with a canal and flowed south towards the town of Waterford.

"This appears to be the perfect spot for our picnic," Beau said, cheerfully picking up the punting pole. He pushed the boat towards shore. "What do you say? We still have the remainder of the day for exploring."

She nodded her head in agreement, realizing that she had developed a small pang of hunger. Tim eagerly jumped out of the boat as it touched the grassy bank and ran around sniffing the neighboring trees and bushes, barking at scurrying squirrels.

Beau, holding the boat's rope, jumped ashore and tied it around the trunk of a tree. She handed him the basket along with the large blanket, which he set aside on the sandy stretch before turning back to help her alight.

Their midday meal did not resemble the elaborate picnics she had previously hosted at Dovehill Hall. The outdoor meals there had been grandiose affairs involving a whole battalion of servants carrying tents, pillows, tables, china plates, silver, throws, and food served piping hot from the hall's kitchen.

Instead, once the tartan blanket was laid out under the shade of a large oak tree, they settled comfortably and enjoyed watching Tim's antics before tucking into the simple, yet delicious fare, which included cold meat pies, sliced cheese, deviled eggs and crisp, tart apples. What a pleasant experience, she mused, sitting in the dappled sunlight seeping through the trees surrounding them. No, she felt more than pleasant, she realized. She felt contentment. A foreign feeling to her and she reveled in it. She remembered the headaches she had previously endured when her husband had hosted picnics. He would become uptight and unpleasant if the slightest detail was amiss. What should have been a pleasant afternoon in the sunshine and fresh air had always turned into a demanding performance. She laid her head back onto her arm with a sigh of contentment.

She didn't have to listen anymore to the prattle of some uppity dowager or pretend to be fascinated by some aged jackanapes's latest tomfoolery. Instead she gazed languidly at the water fowl floating by and the occasional butterfly flit onto a nearby patch of milkweed. Lying here beneath the trees, doing absolutely nothing was pure bliss.

"Is this too rustic for you?" Beau asked, shooing away a fly that landed onto his meat pie. "Perhaps you would prefer to return to Dovehill Hall? I can continue on my own to the cave. You do not have to accompany me."

"No, not at all . . ." she said, a slight edge in her voice, knowing he had not given up trying to convince her to remain at the hall. "It reminds me of what a philosopher once said about the benefits of having a picnic out in the open. Let me see if I can remember the conversation . . . ah yes . . . he called it 'communing'. I suppose this is what we are doing—communing with nature, by simply enjoying it." She did not add that it was not nature that at this moment held her attention, but the enticing gentleman seated next to her.

The manner in which he looked down at her with his sparkling eyes sent her heart hammering with anticipation. Secretly, she wanted to be touched and made love to again by him.

"Do you believe in curses and enchantments?" she asked fingering her brooch, thinking about her husband's death and the banshee's frightening announcement of it.

"I do—although I acknowledge much of it is pure superstition, brought about by the need to explain away some of the misfortunes of life. However, some of the spells one can cast are based upon common sense."

"Common sense spells?" She laughed, thinking of storybook enchantments concerning pixie dust and fortunetelling bones. "How can that be?"

"Hmm . . . let me see . . ." he murmured, plucking at some of the clover growing near him. "Do you know the Irish spell for falling in love?"

"No," she said, barely breathing as he drew closer.

"Oh, it's full of enchantment and common sense," he said. "May I cast the spell upon you, so that you might experience it for yourself?"

"Please do," she whispered.

Silently, she added to herself, *I believe I am already falling under your charm.*

"It's really quite simple. We take some clover like this," he explained, showing her the handful he had plucked. "And then we hold hands for a few minutes, giving the enchantment time to work. Shall we give it a try?"

She nodded an agreement, her eyes never leaving

his. He took her hand into his own. She felt the damp clover between them.

Silently, not saying a word, with his free hand, he gently touched her face. His fingers traced the rounded contour of her cheek and the delicate line of her jaw, then down to her chin, delicately cupping it.

His blue eyes, the color of a clear midnight sky, gazed into hers. Breaching the distance between them, he lowered his face—tenderly touching his lips to hers. With his free hand, he brought her closer to him. Holding her, he kissed her gently, warming her heart.

They broke apart, but their hands remained clasped.

"I now understand what you mean." She breathed, her heart thudding heavily as blood reddened her cheeks. "That was truly enchanting."

"Yes, it was," he said softly in agreement.

If indeed a love spell had been cast, it was the magical meeting of two hearts seeking out their mate. They had discovered the person who was to become both their beloved friend and lover. The person they could count upon to honor, protect, and care for them for the rest of their lives. And it was wonderful.

Chapter 9

Tim, who'd been dashing in and out of the water, reminded them of their original purpose for being there. He came over and dropped the wet stick he carried in his mouth at their feet.

"This is the last time, boy," Beau said, as he picked it up, then flung it towards the boat. They watched as the young pup happily chased after it. Tim's black body quivered with energy. After having taken an afternoon nap, he was ready for the next adventure.

Quickly, Kathleen repacked the wicker basket and folded the tartan blanket, stowing them into the boat. Whistling to the dog to come, Beau helped her step into the craft. After the young animal had reseated himself, the master untied the rope and gave it a gentle shove. They glided back into the deep waters as they continued their journey down the tranquil south shore of the lake.

Thinking themselves alone, they were unaware of three sets of beady, brown eyes watching their every move. The spies were well-hidden by the thick vegetation along the lake's bank, having arrived at the flat knoll undetected by using a narrow footpath that ran parallel to shore.

"Ye had best go on ahead, Ian, and see if they intend to continue," whispered a woman crouched next to a much younger man beside her. "We'll follow from behind. I want to be certain they leave."

"What shall I tell the others?"

"If they discover the treasure's location before us— kill them," she replied coldly. Her dark eyes gleamed dangerously. "We shall make it look like they drowned from a boating accident. No one will be the wiser."

The woman felt joyful at the idea of ridding herself

of the two young people who she hoped would lead her to the treasure. Raised in Urlingford, she had always known of its existence. She thought by living and working in the hall with old Lord Bangford, she would eventually discover its whereabouts.

She thought he would confide in her the secret location of the treasure after she'd befriended him. But years passed and he married that golden-haired chit. Over time he became more stubborn and secretive until it reached a dangerous point.

Her men, bored with hiding in the woods, imposed on the old lord's hospitality. They insisted on being wined and dined at the hall, as if they were gentlemen of the realm. They openly drank barrels of illegal rum and ogled his beautiful wife. The last was an outrage the old lord could not tolerate.

They may use his land, he had later raged at her, but not his home. As a result, he'd wanted nothing more to do with her. He threatened to expose her activities to the authorities. The old goat had dared to threaten her, the most dangerous pirate in Ireland. To think she'd helped to enrich his half-empty pockets! She had no choice but to get rid of him.

One night, during one of the old lord's secret forays, she followed him. When he reached the open stairway by the round monastery tower, she took her opportunity. She crept up from behind and forcefully shoved him backwards.

Arms flailing, he lost his balance and fell into the chapel's stained glass window, splintering it into a million little pieces, and dying a quick but painful death. She'd wanted to retrieve the Druid's brooch from the altar, but the screaming banshee interfered.

She shuddered, remembering the ghostly apparition suddenly hovering over the lifeless body of the dead lord. The spirit was there to collect his soul. And like a jealous lover, the banshee had frightened her away from the dead body and the enchanted brooch.

Fearful that the banshee might claim her soul as well, she had fled and returned to her bedchamber. Once there she ignored the urgent poundings on the door that followed.

The head butler, alarmed by the banshee's screams, cried out to her, "Mrs. O'Grady . . . Mrs. O'Grady . . . are you there? Your assistance is required."

But she did not respond. She kept the door bolted.

It was not until the next day that she made her appearance. She excused her absence by saying she'd taken a sleeping potion before going to bed. She had therefore heard nothing.

Being the head of staff and perceived as loyal to Lord Langtry, her alibi went unquestioned. It had all been quite easy . . . until the reading of the will.

Her co-conspirators, she noted, were shut out of the fortune—those idle aristocrats had not known how to handle their own flesh and blood. For years they had expected her to manage his lordship and find the treasure—a task she had been capable of doing. But then that interfering solicitor took the household keys away from her before she'd had the opportunity to search the dead lord's chambers for the treasure map.

Aye, she decided grimly, she would not mind breaking the handsome solicitor's neck. As for the legacy Lord Bangford left her, what was a modest country house compared to the mountain of treasure she knew was at hand? Nothing but a small token for the years of devoted service and companionship she had given him.

She suspected one of those inbred aristocrats had tried to have that child bride killed. She had heard rumors concerning the attempted assassination of Lady Kathleen in Dublin. The imbeciles had aroused suspicion. The child had ever since been doubly guarded.

However, it did not bring them any nearer to the treasure or to inheriting the hall. From what she learned from her spies, the young widow was in the process of writing a new will. This one would disinherit everyone.

"Damnable nuisances," she muttered under her breath.

She watched the couple continue to float towards the river. She had seen Lord Bangford disappear into the off-shooting tributary before. But she had not come any closer to discovering the secret hiding place. This time, following from behind, she would. They would lead her to the treasure and to their own doom.

The dense growth along the edge of the lake became almost impenetrable. Tim, sensing the intense excitement of his two human companions, became respectfully quiet. His shaggy body no longer quivered when he spied a bird or frog. He sat like a figurehead at the bow of the small boat, completely still.

"We turn here into the river," Beau said, consulting the map. He held the oars and rowed, directing the skiff into the narrower river.

For a moment Kathleen thought she saw movement in the brush. Leaves and twigs shook. But she quickly dismissed the notion that it was a person.

Probably some deer, she told herself.

But the quick hammering of her heart forewarned her to be wary. There was something disquieting about being surrounded by the thick greenery. It was almost as if they were entering a dense trap.

Her senses prickled, but she did not take heed. The treasure was hidden somewhere ahead. Soon they would find it.

The river thinned, but the water was deep enough for their skiff to remain afloat. Plant vegetation sticking out of the water made rowing impossible. Beau stood and taking the punting poll into his hands began to feel his way through the dense growth. She watched as the firm muscles on his arms bulged with effort. From time to time he consulted the map for the hand drawn landmarks for them to follow.

"There . . ." he said, pointing to a rock formation on their left. "A symbol! We must be on the right river."

She turned and looked expectantly up at the underside of a large rock's overhanging ledge. Carved into the surface was the facsimile of the lover's knot. She felt a sense of elation. They were correctly headed towards the treasure's cave.

"How much farther do you suppose?" she asked, tilting her head a little to one side as she read the map.

"We should be coming upon the next to last symbol. It will indicate the route to follow."

"Do you think it's located nearby?"

"Difficult to say . . . we should know in a little bit when we find the next marking. And according to the map that should be soon."

She wondered if perhaps the only way to reach the cave was by boat or if they were to find a footpath and follow it. Some innate sense told her that if they could simply stroll up to the treasure's cave, it would have been found ages ago. No, she suspected, this was going to require a bit of effort on their part.

"Oh, I do hope there aren't any insects," she said aloud.

She shuddered. She detested anything small that had multiple legs, crawled, or worse . . . had wings and flew.

"I cannot promise that there won't be any," he replied. "Once when I was a lad, I explored a cave near the park by my family's home. I had to wade through ankle deep water. When I re-emerged from my expedition, I discovered that I had some unwanted travelers on my legs . . . I was covered in bloodsuckers."

"Oh, how dreadful," she said faintly, picturing the small round parasites.

She could not imagine for a moment what she would do if she encountered them. The thought of pulling off the squishy arthropods made her wince with disgust. But she was resolved, despite her abhorrence of creepy crawlies, not to turn tail and return to the hall. No spider or leech was going to stand in her way. She wanted to see the treasure for herself.

She knew her late husband had compensated being bowlegged by strengthening his upper torso. She had born numerous bruises, which were well-hidden under the long sleeved gowns she wore, because of it. She suspected wherever the treasure was he had rowed there by himself. She knew his character; he had trusted no one.

Once the treasure was found, she would be able to leave all the unpleasant connections associated with Bangford and her uncle in the past. The pirates and the memories of her husband's tyranny would no longer be able to haunt her.

She would at last be free to start a new chapter in her life. Finding the treasure was one more way for her to become independent. Day-by-day, with Beau's help, she had been building a life controlled by only one person . . . herself.

"There . . ." Beau said pointing to the side of a roughly built hut on a small islet in the middle of the river. On the side of the walls was painted the lover's knot. An arrow pointing in the direction they were to turn was stenciled beneath the symbol. He turned the boat, following it.

The river split in two. Suddenly, the water churned faster as a strong current pushed them forward. She thought uneasily how simple it would be to drown if the boat should suddenly capsize. The swift undertow would pull them under in the blink of an eye.

Beverly Adam

She shivered, frightened at the thought.

"Are you cold?" he asked, noticing.

He had reseated himself in the pilot's seat. The river had cleared of vegetation and he was able to steer with the rudder. "Would you like me to drape the blanket over your shoulders?"

She shook her head.

"It's not that. I am afraid I'm letting all my childhood fears haunt me today," she confessed sheepishly. "First the thought of spiders—and now being surrounded by this deep water . . . it reminds me that I am not a good swimmer. Although mind, my governess insisted I learn how to swim. I do not however, have the ability to pass myself off as a mermaid. Are you comfortable in the water?"

"I cannot claim to be a son of Poseidon. But I did attend a school where one of the required rituals was to bathe in the frigid waters of the sea. My headmaster had a rather Spartan attitude towards our health. I consider it to be one of life's little miracles that I did not contract lung fever during that time. Oddly enough, after I finished my studies, I kept up the habit of occasionally dipping into frigid waters."

She looked at his tall frame and tried to picture him diving into a local pond. Perhaps he would swim during a moonlit night when no one was around? His waist was small and his long legs covered in tan breech trousers were firm. She recalled seeing him ride in the early morning around Dovehill Hall. She had observed for herself how muscular he was. Her cheeks warmed at the remembrance of seeing him naked during their lovemaking.

He had resembled the handsome Roman statue of the hero Hercules. Beau was solidly built with beautifully defined muscles and a manly broad torso. A handsome face and confident attitude completed his features, like the demigod the Spartans claimed was their first king, he was a born warrior. Aye, if the Spartans had chosen one of their own to carve into a stone, he undoubtedly would have looked like him, she decided. And she was certain the women of the Spartan village would have swooned at the very sight.

The vegetation thickened again, forcing Beau to use the punting pole. Oddly enough a large rock lay flat across two others. She made careful note of it. "It looks like a Druid symbol," she remarked. She looked down at the map. "According to this, those three stones comprise an altar."

"The Druids probably used it for offerings, following this river to the cave," he responded. "They may have used it for important rituals."

"Fascinating . . ." she murmured. Her eagerness to see this mysterious place was increasing by the minute. It was becoming a veritable Aladdin's cave of unexpected wonders.

"Do you think there will be any signs which will be able to tell us anything about the Druids? They were such an ancient people, and so little is known about them."

"If we are fortunate, there may be," he agreed, cheerfully. "We shall have to wait and see. In due time the cave and all its hidden treasures will be revealed."

She traced the route they were following with her finger. Another significant marking was indicated on the map.

"There ought to be a large walnut tree appearing soon . . . after which we enter a small stream that will take us straight into the cave."

"Ah, I see it," said Beau. "It's directly ahead."

"I've never seen one so large before." She breathed, admiring the tree's wide girth. Five people holding out their arms could have surrounded the trunk. They passed beneath its massive branches that cast a large shadow over them. She looked up at the tree, easily picturing ancient Celts perched above her. "It must be thousands of years old . . . remarkable."

"There's the mark again," he said. He pointed to a smooth rock near the foot of the tree's roots. On the stone was etched the lover's knot.

The boat glided into a narrow stream. Tall water grass brushed up against the small craft on both sides. He guided it through the narrow channel and touched the stream's bottom with the punting pole.

"Is it deep enough for us to continue?" she asked, not looking forward to being forced to turn around.

"For now," he said, nodding his head. "I think we can continue on as we have, without getting our feet wet."

A solid wall of rock now hemmed them in on each side. They rowed very close to the stone. If she reached out her hand, she could touch the moss and ferns that grew on the lower outcropping of the ledges.

If they hadn't been looking for the next marking, they would have easily missed the cave entrance. It appeared on the bottom edge of the left wall. The opening itself blended into the stone. It was at a sharp cornered angle, which from a stone's throw away could not be seen with the naked eye.

"How easy it would have been for us to row past it," she commented upon sighting the marking. "If it was not for the map, we would not have known where to look."

The mouth of the cave was a narrow slit just large enough for the boat to enter. The roof was of solid rock. It grew proportionally larger the farther they traveled. They could hear the sound of rushing water ahead of them.

"The falls," he remarked. "I remember seeing it marked next to the treasure chest on the map. Apparently there is an underground river, which interconnects with this cave and flows out to join the main river. At one time it must have been a raging torrent and hollowed out these stone walls."

He continued to row them farther into the cave's mouth. Stalactites hung in a white gray icicle-shaped fashion from the roof. They dripped occasional drops of water into the stream. Some stalagmite minerals grew pointedly upwards, resembling sharp teeth, created by the shallows of wet lime stone nearby.

"How interesting . . ." she remarked, looking at groups of stalactites that resembled a long column. "It's almost Roman in shape, like a miniature temple."

They reached the point where the waterfall rushed downwards to reach the cave's stream. A rainbow formed from its mist. There appeared to be no need for lanterns. There were large gaping holes in the ceiling, providing ample daylight.

It was only as they neared the end of the cave that they noticed any discernible traces of the ancient Druids who once used it for their sacred rituals. There was a sandy bank on their right. On the cave wall behind it was a mural of primitive drawings.

Red spirals, pictures of small animals and people were drawn on the stone. It was charred black by soot from pit fires. The hand-drawn pictures curved across the wall. They were predominantly painted in colors of red-berry ink, with outlines in black charcoal.

"They probably did animal sacrifices here to their gods," he said, nodding his head at what appeared to be a large fire pit.

"It appears that they may have believed that once a person died, his soul transferred itself into another, thus never truly ending, going on for eternity. They may have possibly believed they were morphing into an animal or another person, as a type of reincarnation. It's a bit difficult to tell by these pictures. I have a scholarly friend in Dublin who is making a study of cave drawings similar to these on the west coast. We studied Greek together in college."

"That is astonishing . . . you must invite him to visit when we return. I should very much like him to examine the ones here. It would be enlightening to hear his interpretation behind their meaning, if there should be any."

"I'll write to him when we return to the hall," he agreed, admiring the primitive picture of a herd of deer painted in red.

He brought the boat up to the shore and anchored it. Gallantly, he stood in the knee-deep water tying the rope. Putting his hands on her waist, he said, "May I bring you ashore, my lady? I wouldn't want you to get your feet wet."

"Thank you. Are you certain I won't be too heavy for you?" she asked a little anxious.

"Not a bit. You'll be as light as a feather." And without any further ado, he lifted her into his arms.

She placed her hands on his strong shoulders, feeling his muscles tighten beneath her finger tips. She felt a secret delight. It was reminiscent of her happy childhood when she was carried to bed. A feeling of security, an emotion she had never thought to experience again, pervaded her being.

Gently, he set her down. A look passed between them. It was the unspoken connection of two people who were drawn to each other, enjoying the other's company as they shared a moment of happy solitude.

The pebbled sand crunched beneath her feet as she walked towards the fire pit. Kathleen felt a tingle of excitement run down her spine at the knowledge that the treasure was nearby. In a few moments she would be able to touch it. The pictographs on the wall had been an exciting find, but now she would actually hold history in her hands.

Thoughtfully, she touched her brooch. Hopefully, they would find more items like this in the treasure chest. *But undoubtedly no matter what we find, it will be valuable in our eyes because we discovered it together,* she decided.

She looked over at Beau as he stood next to her. She realized she had come to fully trust him. Any other man might have taken the treasure and left her with nothing, but not him. They would find the treasure chest together. She knew he would not betray her.

She had been worried about his integrity, when he had first become her guardian. Was he truly what he appeared to be? Would he betray her? But now she knew the answers . . . he had proven himself.

When he stood up for her and removed the dominating Mrs. O'Grady from her post, she knew then he could be depended upon. But she had held some doubt. However, he had over the past few weeks become her confidante, friend, protector, and finally her lover.

It was with great satisfaction she realized what that meant. She completely trusted him. She no longer had any doubts about his loyalty. It was a revelation that caused her heart to pound happily. She both loved and trusted him. And soon she would tell him.

Beau looked at the map and said, "The treasure is over here."

He walked over to the fire pit. Crouching, he proceeded to dig around the burnt wood and charred sand with a shovel. A metal handle surfaced from out of the sooty ground.

Eagerly, she helped dig around what now appeared to be a wooden container. The round lid with its metal studs and straps became visible. More digging revealed the four, sharp edges and the slated sides of a large wooden chest.

Its size explained why her late husband had not been able to remove it from the pit. It would have required a very strong man to do so. And as her husband was an invalid, he had not been able to move it. So he had left it hidden in the cave.

Bracing his legs on each side of the pit, Beau lifted. Ashy soot and sand fell away from the box as he slowly hefted the chest up from its burial place. He set it on the edge of the hole. Wiping his brow, he grinned at her.

"We did it." She breathed.

Her heart pounded with excitement. They had found the treasure. It was real. She examined it. The large metal padlock attached to the side was unusual. The tumbler's design was circular instead of triangular. Yet it had a familiar look.

"Your brooch," Beau said, looking at her shawl. "It may be the key to opening it."

She nodded her head in agreement, recognizing the familiar shape. Carefully, she placed the face of the jewel inside the tumbler. It fit perfectly. But the lock did not budge.

"Try turning it," he suggested.

She did so, gently moving it to the right. A satisfying *click* was heard. The pin moved. The lock sprung open.

Lifting the heavy lid, they discovered the treasure.

Inside, gems of every size and description filled the chest to the brim. Necklaces made of pearls, amethysts, heavy chains of finely wrought silver and pounded gold embedded with rubies and topazes lay inside. Medieval artifacts of goblets, crosses, amulets, bracelets, rings, and the heads of small statues of Druid gods, stuck out of the top of the impressive pile.

They hugged, smiling with happiness over the find. Filled with excitement, they kissed. Their mutual joy over the discovery ignited a bonding flame between them. They had been successful in their quest.

Chapter 10

Beau placed the treasure in the boat. They had already decided to have archeological experts help them identify the treasure's objects. They wanted to know the origins of the jewels and valuable artifacts and then they would decide how to distribute them.

Believing that she already had enough wealth to take care of her needs, Kathleen resolved not to sell off any of the antiquities. Instead, she would donate them to deserving universities and museums involved in studying medieval and early Irish culture. She did not know it, but an entire wing of a museum would later be named in her honor.

When they were prepared to return to Dovehill Hall, Tim, with some reluctance, parted with a treasure as well . . . a deer bone he had discovered in the ancient fire pit. She refused to let him carry it aboard.

"You will get ash all over yourself and us," she said to the woeful animal. "But if you are good, I will give you another one when we return." As if he understood, the pet reluctantly dropped the prize and took his habitual place at the bow.

Smiling at the exchange, Beau lifted the anchor and began to row them back to the river.

Passing the falls, she could not help but think of the banshee and of the brooch she wore . . . the death of her husband had brought her here. It had also brought Beau back into her life—creating a new beginning for her.

Something good had come out of all the sorrow she had endured since her parents' deaths. Looking at the waterfall's rainbow, she realized they had found the legendary treasure at the end of it.

Fingering the lover's knot, she mused, *Perhaps the*

banshee left the brooch for me to find? Maybe she had wanted me to discover the treasure? But she knew it was more than that. She glanced over at Beau as he rowed. Her heart lifted at the sight of him. Perhaps the banshee had desired to help her find love, as well?

Once they had departed from the cave, Beau turned their boat towards the narrow river. They passed the solid stone walls peacefully, unaware that their arrival was anticipated. As they entered the river leading back to the lake, her flesh prickled with goose bumps of awareness. She sensed they were no longer alone. Unseen eyes were upon them.

Tim growled. His mouth trembled into a snarl. He too sensed a disquieting presence. The hair on the back of his neck bristled.

"Easy, boy," Beau said, giving the dog a reassuring pat. He put a restraining hand on the dog's leash. He looked uneasily about him.

"We are being followed, aren't we?" she asked in a half whisper.

Silently, he nodded. He opened his coat, inside, strapped to his hips and under his arms, were shooting pistols.

Her eyes widened at the sight of them.

"Ever since the attack in Dublin, they have not left my side. Whoever is out there must have been waiting for us. Undoubtedly they want the treasure."

She shuddered as two rough looking men appeared out of the thick brush. An older woman stood next to them. She recognized her.

"It's Mrs. O'Grady!" She breathed, but her relief at the sight of the solemn-faced servant was short-lived. The older woman and the two men aimed long firing pistols at them.

"What shall we do?" she asked, biting down on her lip in worry.

"Hopefully, we'll be able to out-race them to the

lake," he said. "There, we can summon help from shore. Until then we'll have to try and remain out of reach."

He handed her the torn end of Tim's leash.

"You had best hold onto this while I steer. I'm afraid he'll jump out of the boat and try to attack them."

Silently, she took it from him, gripping the frayed end with all her might. She was determined that this time no harm would come to her brave pet.

"Calm, Tim . . . calm . . ." she said soothingly, stroking him.

Warily, she eyed the shore. She caught glimpses of their pursuers as they ran along the footpath. She watched as they pushed through the dense growth.

The water's clarity changed from murky to clear, the current now ran swiftly as they left the narrow vegetation filled river. Leaves and branches floated past. The brush thinned. Their pursuers would now be able to get a clear aim at them.

Beau directed the small skiff into the wider river. She noticed he tried to keep the craft in the center, away from the shore. She could see the thieves clearly through the thin brush, taking aim . . .

They began firing off their weapons, setting Tim into a frenzy of barking. He pulled on the rope in an effort to lunge out of the boat, his fangs bared. Kathleen held on tight. If the dog jumped out, he would drown.

She noticed the shots were not aimed at hitting them, but rather at the bottom of their craft. The pirates peppered the water with shots. A pair of white ducks squawked in protest, paddling swiftly away.

Her heart pounded wildly with the sudden realization that the villains intended to sink them. If they ended up in the water, the swift current's undertow would undoubtedly pull them under. They would drown, saving the pirates the trouble of killing them.

Once they were disposed of, the pirates would search

for the treasure chest with long grappling hooks. It was a dubious enterprise. The chest might be carried away or spill out onto the muddy bottom and be lost forever, but the heartless criminals appeared to be willing to take the risk.

"Now we're in for it," commented Beau grimly as the current began to slow.

They had reached the mouth of the lake. "Do you think you can handle both the rudder and Tim? I am going to try and fire off a couple of shots to hold them back."

She nodded and dragged the barking dog to the opposite side.

Beau removed one of the revolvers, carefully checking the flintlock before taking aim. None of his powder or shot was to be wasted. He would make certain that each firing counted.

He extended his arm and took aim. He had dueled against several discontented losers, after defeating them in court, fought off robbers who once tried to invade his country house in Tipperary, and helped his friend retrieve his kidnapped bride from cutthroat mercenaries. He handled himself with the steady *sang froid* only a gentleman used to handling weapons in the most dangerous of circumstances could do . . . he fired.

They heard a cry as the pirate standing on the right side of Mrs. O'Grady was hit. After the smoke cleared, they could see the man clutching his thigh where he'd been shot. The pirate swore vehemently.

"Kill them!" the bleeding man ordered. "Kill them!"

"No, Ian," said Mrs. O' Grady firmly, putting out a restraining arm to stop them from shooting. "It has to look like an accident. It must appear as if they drowned. If they're shot and killed, the authorities will be onto us. We could lose everything if we're discovered."

Beau reloaded the firing pistol, aimed once more, and fired. This time it grazed a tree, an inch to the right of the other pirate's head, sending splinters of bark flying everywhere. The villains ducked, hiding in the shelter of the thicket as they fired off a round of avenging shots. Kathleen could see in the near distance the lake spreading out before them. They had only a few more yards to go before reaching it.

"Don't worry, lad. We'll make it," she said to Tim reassuringly.

His large brown eyes looked trustingly up at her. She had forced him to lie down, fearing he might be hit by one of the stray bullets.

The pirates also realized their prize was about to escape. They ran along the edge of the riverbank in a futile effort to stop them. But it was too late. Beau urged the boat onward using his punting pole, giving it added momentum. Soon they were in the middle of the lake. The deep water was dark and the weather above matched its color, pitch black with heavy rain clouds.

Worried, she searched the shore for their pursuers. She knew they would not be far behind. Those greedy cutthroats were not going to let them escape.

"We'll head for the hall. I'll fire off a couple of rounds, alerting those ashore that we're in distress. That ought to bring a rescue boat to us and give added protection. They wouldn't dare kill us in front of witnesses."

As Beau spoke, Kathleen noticed a small craft entering from the mouth of the subsidiary river they had just left. Three people were on board.

"It's them," she said with a tiny quiver of fear. The black poker bonnet Mrs. O'Grady habitually wore was noticeable from a distance.

"Aye, they're in hot pursuit. They probably think they can capture us before we reach the other side. We'll have to try and outrun them," Beau said.

He took an oar and handed it to her. They began to row

in unison, trying to outdistance their pursuers. Tim started barking upon sighting the villains closing in on them. Fortunately, they were already several yards ahead. The shots fired in their direction sank uselessly into the lake.

When they neared Dovehill Hall's shore, Beau raised his pistols and fired off two shots. A young lad herding a flock nearby sighted them. Kathleen waved a white handkerchief in the air to show they were in distress.

With a cry of alarm, the lad turned and ran off in search of help.

"That should get things started," Beau muttered with satisfaction.

The pirates started firing indiscriminately, letting their baser instincts reign, fearing their valuable prize was about to slip away. The lake was too deep to attempt any type of salvaging, but the villains were desperate. The loss of the treasure was unacceptable.

Servants came running from the hall. They shouted out to them, waving aprons. Several of the men hurriedly untied a nearby fishing boat and began to row out to them.

Kathleen recognized Beau's manservant, Humphrey, among them. She felt like cheering. They were going to be rescued.

"Over here!" she shouted, waving her hands in the air.

The boat bobbed roughly up and down. She felt the pit of her stomach fall as the water turned choppy. The boat lurched dangerously to one side.

"Careful, or we'll tip," warned Beau.

Realizing he was right, she stilled her movements. *The villains must stand down,* she told herself reassuringly, holding onto the sides. *They cannot continue this mad pursuit and risk being caught or killed.*

The grim faces of the pirates were plainly visible, their anger and frustration etched on their scowling faces. Murderous intent shone in their eyes as they fired off their weapons for the last time.

Several of the shots hit the boat. A trickle of water began to enter. A return volley was heard from their rescuers. A loud cry was heard from the pirates. One of Humphrey's shots hit the man closest to the stern, squarely in the chest, the same one who'd been wounded earlier in the thigh. The villain fell forward, blood seeping through his shirt. Kathleen could see Humphrey and the others hurriedly reloading.

"Well done, Humphrey," said Beau approvingly.

The pirates, realizing they were about to be outnumbered, made a hasty retreat back towards the river inlet. Sooner than you can say, *Jack your brother*, their rescuers' boat pulled up alongside their leaking skiff.

Beau reached out enthusiastically, shaking their rescuers' hands, smiling broadly at Humphrey and the others.

"Demme . . . if I'm not happy to see you, gentlemen," he said. "I thought there for a moment those sharks would soon be discovering a different sort of fish to sharpen their fangs upon."

"They never stood a chance," Kathleen put in, remembering the pirate he wounded. "They were too terrified of being torn in two by you. And when Humphrey shot one of them, they turned tail. Aye, they dared not stay any longer when you brave gentlemen came swiftly to our rescue."

"Please, say no more of this, Lady Langtry. You will be shaming us for not reaching you and Master Powers sooner," said Humphrey in a gruff manner. Although she could tell he was nonetheless pleased by her heartfelt compliments.

"Have the militia been sent for?" Beau asked.

"Aye, we sent Tommy to fetch them and the village

constable as soon as we saw the trouble you were in," his manservant replied. "We want to make certain those pirates reach hell safely. . . And to think that damnable Mrs. O'Grady turned out to be one of them. It quite makes one's blood boil."

"Aye, that it does," said Beau in agreement, thoughtfully looking at Kathleen.

She could tell he was silently wondering how she felt about the matter. How did this revelation of close betrayal affect her?

She'd been forced to endure the housekeeper's dominating interference many times over the past two years. The black-hearted villainess had used Dovehill Hall to hide her illegal activities as a smuggler. It might have continued unchecked if Lord Langtry hadn't suddenly died and left the entire estate to Kathleen.

"Mrs. O'Grady will undoubtedly be justly rewarded one day by the devil himself for her wrong doings," she said out loud, answering the unasked question. "If the authorities catch her and those wicked men, they will face the full penalty of the law. That will satisfy any revenge I could possibly wish upon them."

"For certain, that it will. May justice rule," agreed the handsome magistrate.

Although she noted he lightly fingered the weapon in his hand, he was undoubtedly thinking of the justice he would like to have personally enacted upon the pirates who had dared to try and harm them.

* * *

They returned peacefully to Dovehill Hall. Their boat was tethered to their rescuers' as it was feared it might sink. Upon reaching shore, they were greeted by servants and village locals. A few of them had taken the precaution of carrying weapons in case the pirates dared to return.

"Tim, heel." she urged the dog that, from the moment his paws touched ground, wanted to chase after the scoundrels.

His dark whiskered snout in the air, the black Lab motionlessly pointed. One leg was elegantly lifted, as the hall's huntsmen had trained him to do. He was prepared to sniff the villains out for them.

"What a good little fellow you have there, Lady Langtry," said the village constable, approvingly.

The constable, or *guarda,* as he was known, noticed the dog's reaction. A thoughtful look passed between him and the local militia's captain.

"Might we use him to ferret out these dangerous miscreants, ma'am?"

She hesitated. On one hand, she wanted the villains to be caught, but on the other, she did not want to risk Tim being hurt again.

"I will go with them," said Beau wisely, sensing her uncertainty. "In this manner, we may be rest assured no harm will come to him. That would be agreeable with you, wouldn't it, Constable?"

"Aye, sir, it would no doubt be better for the lad to have his master accompany us on the hunt," the guarda readily agreed. "For sure, he'll be more manageable that way."

She nodded and said, "Then it's agreed, but I am coming along, as well."

"But Kathleen—" Beau protested. They had nearly lost their lives.

"Tim is my dog," she cut in. "I know I am being stubborn. But I would never be able to forgive myself if anything happened to him."

Frustrated, Beau swore under his breath. But when he looked at her, the determination in her wide eyes and the firm set of her jaw told him she would not back down.

"Very well," he relented. "But you are to remain in the rear with the militia. Understood?"

"But I—"

"Agree, Kathleen, or back to the hall you go."

She could tell by the look in his eyes and the stern determination in his voice he meant his words. She had a feeling he would physically take her back if she didn't agree. Silently, she nodded.

They searched along the lake's shore. Beau held Tim's leash at the head of the line as the militia spread out, searching the overgrowth for the pirates. Kathleen kept up as best she could. Her walking clothes were not made for dealing with brambles and sharp thorns. Impatiently, she had to stop several times and unhook her long skirts from catching vines.

With his large paws, Tim ran easily through the thicket in his eagerness to chase after the pirates. She could see Beau valiantly hanging onto the end of the leash as he tried to keep up with the young dog. They finally reached the river's inlet shore. Tim gave a sharp bark and pointed.

"Good boy! Well done," praised Beau, patting Tim's head.

Kathleen walked up the militia line and stood beside them. She was curious to see what he had found. Dark patches of blood lay splattered around on the ground.

"Do you know how many of them were wounded?" asked the constable.

"One was, quite badly," she supplied, recalling their earlier encounter. "He was shot in the thigh and the chest."

"Aye, then they can't be too far off." He nodded. "We should be able to catch up with them quickly."

"Come on, boy," murmured Beau encouragingly to the Lab, easing the leash he held.

Tim, as if understanding, gave a short bark and set

off. His long plumed tail wagged like a flag to follow.

A bit farther, almost completely submerged, they came upon the boat the pirates and Mrs. O'Grady were last seen in. It had sunk. The hull now lay in the river.

"Don't get too near the edge," advised Beau. "The current, as you can see, is quite dangerous here. It may be they all drowned."

"Aye, that is so," agreed the constable, speaking to the head officer in charge of the militia. "Captain, I'd pass word on to your men to be careful."

The captain gave a silent salute and went after his soldiers to warn them of the possible danger. Tim, not the least bit distracted by the submerged vessel, sniffed around nearby. His body tensed and he gave a few sharp barks, lifting his paw, pointing.

"What have you found, boy?" Beau asked softly.

Quietly, he walked up to the side of the animal. He pulled back the low branch that dangled over the edge of the river. Lying on the ground partially in the water was the pirate Humphrey had shot.

The pirate wasn't moving. A horrible stench emitted from him as midges swarmed around his body. He was dead—his life had bled out of him.

Chapter 11

The search for the remaining pirates ceased at sunset. The darkness made it impossible to continue. A few of the militia camped near Dovehill Hall. The soldiers were posted on watch as a precaution against the pirates returning.

Kathleen could see the campfires along the shore of the lake from a window in the dining room. It was a reassuring sight. She was still recovering from the horrible discovery of the dead pirate's body.

She shuddered at the memory. The smell of the decaying body had been stomach clenching. The sight of him lying there under the brush, his sightless, glassy eyes staring up at them, was unforgettable. He served as a reminder of how close she had come to death.

Someone gently knocked on the door.

The newly appointed housekeeper, a young, competent woman in her early thirties, entered. She smiled and curtsied.

"Are you ready for dinner to be served, your ladyship?" she asked.

Kathleen nodded. "You may proceed, Mrs. Cameron. It would appear there will be just the two of us tonight."

She had invited the captain and the constable to dine with them but both had politely declined. They cited their more urgent need to meet with the local priest to make burial arrangements for the dead pirate and to discuss what tactics to take in finding his accomplices.

"Those two scoundrels are still out there," said the guarda, his voice sharp with his desire for action. "And I for one will not rest easy until they are caught and punished for their terrible crimes."

"Aye, that they will be." The captain of the local guard nodded in agreement, one of the rare times he was in complete accord with his Irish counterpart. "We must remain vigilant until these villains are apprehended. Who knows what desperate act they might perpetrate next?"

Those dire warnings ran through her thoughts as she and Beau sat at the candlelit walnut table. She looked over at her dinner companion seated beside her.

If it were not for the brace of arms he kept by his side, Beau appeared to have calmly put the harrowing incidents of the day completely out of his thoughts. They exchanged pleasant conversation, discussing their plans for Dovehill Hall and the final changes to her will.

If for some unforeseen reason she should die, the estate would now pass into the hands of various charities and be run by a designated trusteeship. None of her late husband's relations would be able to make any legal claims. Beau had made certain of that.

They had for the past week been living alone at Dovehill Hall. Lady Fitzpatrick had returned to her own home to take up residence. Kathleen thought fondly of the tiny Irish woman who had served for several weeks as her devoted companion. She had become as dear a friend as Beau had become.

She cast a glance over at the handsome man seated next to her. At the thought of how close they had come to losing their own lives, her heart tightened. She could not imagine how empty her life would be if he should suddenly disappear from it.

Beau had become someone she could count upon. He had been beside her at the most difficult of times, helping and protecting. His opinion and wisdom had guided her through a thick quagmire of expectations and responsibilities. He had aided her with each task, enabling her to slowly become more confident as mistress of a large estate. Because of his mentoring, she was now able to make the important day-to-day decisions concerning the running of Dovehill Hall and its surrounding lands.

She ruled her life and property as she chose. She had only herself to answer to because of him. She knew she owed her current independence to him. He had proved himself and gained her trust and become her lover. As a result, she had fallen in love with him.

Beau abruptly stopped speaking. He turned towards her, an expression of concern on his face. His blue eyes focused on her.

"What is troubling you, Kathleen?" he asked. "I do not believe you heard a word I just said. If you are tired, we can discuss this at another time. The day's events have been rather arduous and draining."

"It's not that," she softly admitted. "I've come to realize something which is both disturbing and wonderful at the same time."

"What is that?"

"Those pirates might have killed you."

He raised his golden eyebrows at her remark. She held a hand up, preventing him from speaking.

"And I cannot bear the thought of you being taken away from me," she continued, her large, china blues eyes fixed upon him. "Such a possibility is most painful to me. I know that if someone were to attack me, you would selflessly place yourself in harm's way. You might possibly be killed by doing so."

"I see," he replied, an amused grin lifting the corner of his lips, "and this is wonderful? I don't understand."

"Yes," she nodded, "because I know I can trust you with my life, and I have never before been able to do that with anyone. There has been no one with whom I could have any confidence in. I have been completely alone and unprotected."

"And now you trust me?"

She nodded. "Yes."

He sat a moment in silence, letting her words sink in. The beautiful woman seated before him had paid him a great compliment. She had faith in him. He recalled their first interview. He remembered the astonished look on her face when he announced he was to become her guardian.

She had been doubtful and afraid, fearing he would be like the other men in her life. She had worried that he would take advantage of her. But he had proven her fears to be unwarranted and their relationship had slowly transformed.

The dangerous events of the last month and the discovery of the treasure had brought them closer together. He'd proven himself. She now trusted him enough to speak openly and without any fear.

He felt a surge of happiness. He'd been hoping she would grow to trust him, but this was unexpected. She had complete faith in him and he knew he would never betray it.

Before he could respond, the sound of gunfire outside startled them.

"What's going on?" she asked.

He went to the window and looked out. More shots were heard. In the dark, he could see nothing. Suddenly, several figures rushed by the window. Shouts followed.

"Stay here," Beau said. "I'll find out what happened."

He picked up his brace of arms and with a determined stride, headed towards the door. She went to him as he reached for the handle.

"You don't suppose the pirates have returned?" she asked, biting down on her lower lip with worry.

"Aye, I do . . . those three did not work this black-market scheme by themselves. It would not surprise me if they came back with a boatload of reinforcements. I think it's best if you remain here where it's safe. Secure the doors after me."

She nodded in agreement and did what he asked, but this decision was a grave error they would both later regret.

Chapter 12

Kathleen and Beau were not the only ones to hear the gunshots. Seated in a pony cart on a road that ran along Dovehill Lake, Lady Agnes heard the shots, as well. She gripped tightly the leather ribbons in her hands as the pony in front of her nervously whinnied.

"Calm yourself, Marigold," she said as much to the animal as herself. "If something is amiss at Dovehill, we must go there at once and offer our assistance."

She touched her favorite sturdy parasol as it lay next to her. In the past, onboard her husband's ship, The Blue Star, she had wielded it with some effect upon the heads of loutish men. She wondered briefly if tonight she would again be forced to do so.

Not frightened by the possibility of putting herself in danger, she turned the pony towards the gothic manse. She noted the scurrying of dark figures along the edge of the lawn leading down to the lake.

"Pirates!" she half exclaimed to herself. Red-coated soldiers ran after them and occasional orders were shouted out.

She halted her cart and hurriedly descended, tying the lead reins to a hitching post.

"You'll have to stay here, while I investigate," she said, gently patting the pony while firmly gripping her parasol.

She headed towards the lake where the dark figures had run. Perhaps she would be able to report back to the militia captain where the pirates were headed?

At the edge of the water, a gray-haired man was seated on the shore. His hands were tied behind his back while another, a pirate in a red-knitted cap, stood nearby smoking, observing the action taking place farther up the hill.

"A prisoner," she whispered to herself, noticing that the gentleman was in a battered merchant captain's uniform.

There was something vaguely familiar about the shape of the man's build. The way he tilted his head and the manner in which his shoulders lay back, but it was only when she crept close enough to see his bearded face, and bright gray blue eyes that her heart leapt with recognition.

It was her husband . . . Captain James William Fitzpatrick!

She let out an involuntary gasp, her heart pounding with joy. She could not believe her eyes. It was her beloved husband—James! He who was missing, thought by many to have drowned at sea with his ship and crew off the coast of an uncharted part of Africa. He was the pirates' prisoner!

She wanted to run to him, to take him into her arms, to kiss him, to tell him she had never stopped searching for him, and never ever let him go, but she halted her first impulsive step towards him upon espying the pirate sentry's assortment of lethal weapons dangling from his belt. She had to deal with him first.

Dressed from head to toe in widow's weeds, she had gone unnoticed down to the shore. Blending into the dark hedge, she quietly skirted the open lawn that sloped gradually to the lake. Her long black shawl covered her head, effectively camouflaging her actions.

Carefully, she crept up behind the pirate sentry. She wanted to get as close as possible to him without being detected.

Rising up suddenly out of the concealing hedge, like a small banshee, Agnes raised her parasol. Her shawl, fluttered in the cool night breeze, resembling the dark wings of a small vengeful angel.

"Have mercy on me!" cried the pirate, frightened,

believing her to be the spirit of death come to claim his wicked soul.

"Take that, you good for nothing bilge rat!" shouted Agnes, furious at the idea that this low-life scum was preventing her husband from returning to her. How dare they keep the finest man in the world captive!

Using both hands, she struck down with all the force she could muster and hit the pirate soundly on the head with the metal stays of her parasol, knocking him out.

"Agnes!" exclaimed James, seeing that his rescuer was none other than his own beloved wife. He closed his eyes and then reopened them again to be certain that she was not a dream, one he had dreamt of during the many lonely nights he'd experienced during the past three years.

Quickly unbinding the ropes that held him, Agnes crouched down to her husband, unable to resist touching his face and kissing his mouth as she did so, trembling with eager anticipation of holding him in her arms once again.

Once his arms were free, he clasped her to him. His hands trembled as they reached up to pull back the heavy widow's weeds that obscured her face, and like a bride on her wedding day, he kissed his devoted wife as if it was the very first time.

* * *

The minutes passed slowly as Kathleen was forced to remain in the dining room wondering what was happening around her. The occasional sound of guns being fired caused her to jump.

Nervously, she peered out the window. Silence reigned—she could sense no movement outside. She anxiously hoped Beau was safe and would return to her, but that didn't occur. Instead, a hand reached up from behind and pulled her backwards.

Frightened, she let out a terrified scream.

"You'd thought I'd gone, didn't you?" said the rasping woman's voice behind her.

Kathleen's arms were viciously pulled.

She winced in pain. Her back had been turned to the bookshelves by the fireplace. She hadn't noticed when someone gently pushed the bookcase forward, as the sound was muffled by the fire crackling in the grate. A secret door leading to a hidden passageway had sprung open.

"Didn't think I would return and seek my revenge, neither," the voice continued.

A sinking feeling of dread filled her being. She recognized the voice and the woman who now forcefully held her.

It was Mrs. O'Grady. She'd returned. And it was obvious she wanted revenge.

"That old fool . . . we all could have been rich. But he didn't want his precious child bride to know about any of his dirty little secrets." O'Grady sneered in contempt at Kathleen's obvious ignorance. "He never told you about his unholy alliance with a bunch of black-market pirates, did he? Or how he'd been harboring us when the redcoats caught wind of our whereabouts?"

Silently, horrified, she shook her head.

Not until her husband's death did she have any knowledge about what was going on under her very nose. He'd kept her blissfully ignorant. She knew nothing of Bangford's dealings with the pirates or about the true character of this evil woman who'd constantly shadowed her.

The older woman chortled, "The old codger didn't want his precious bride to run away. If he could have, he would've kept ye under lock and key. He was frightened that you would betray him. So he never told you anything."

She laughed gloatingly. "Instead, he had me spy on

you. He wanted to make certain you had no control. And that's why he never told you about the passageway, the treasure, or about the black-market goods . . . but now ye know."

The pirate shrugged, keeping a tight grip on her arms, as if all of this were inevitable.

"So you'll have to die," she rasped in satisfaction, as if Kathleen's death was an event she'd been looking forward to.

"You already tried to kill me once," Kathleen hissed, remembering the attempt on her life in Dublin, "and you didn't succeed. You won't this time, either. I will survive and live to see you hanged."

That is if I am able to gain more time, she added to herself. *And come up with a plan to escape her.*

She remembered the vow she'd made to herself in Dublin. She refused to be manipulated like a hopeless pawn by these murderous villains. She would fight for her life.

"Bah." O'Grady spat. "It was not I who tried to have you shot, if that's what you're thinking. It was one of them loathsome cur who his dead lordship called relations. It was them who tried. They wanted you out of the way, so they could inherit the estate and find the treasure for themselves."

"And what of my uncle?" she asked. She glared at the woman.

She hadn't forgotten her dead relation. It was true Uncle Lynch had been a greedy man, but he'd never done this woman any harm, so why had he been killed?

"Was that their doing, as well? Did they have him murdered?"

"Aye, they did," said the ex-housekeeper in a matter-of-fact manner. "That popinjay kept trying to blackmail that high almighty countess and her worthless son into giving him blunt. He bragged that he could get you to do anything he wished. But he failed. And they decided to make certain he never inherited another farthing. They hired one of my mercenaries, Ian, the one who lies dead in yonder churchyard, to kill him. He did a bang up job, didn't he?"

Kathleen shuddered, remembering the open-eyed stare of the dead man.

In the end, the mercenary pirate had received his just reward. He would no longer be troubling the decent inhabitants of the world. His body was good and buried in the ground. And his soul, no doubt, was shaking hands with the devil, in hell.

"What do you plan to do with me?" she asked, knowing the vengeful woman had not come simply to kill her, or she would have already done so by now. There had to be another motive to her kidnapping. What was it?

"My men and I are after seeking what remains of our cargo. You may have snagged the treasure, but we don't intend to leave Ireland empty-handed. Even if a whole regiment of redcoats should come chasing after us." O'Grady snarled. "And to do that, I shall need you. As our hostage, you'll be our protection against being killed by the militia's bayonets."

The female pirate looked her over from head to toe and nodded.

"Aye, they'll not want to shoot us once they spot you. No one will want to accidentally kill the beautiful widow of Dovehill Hall. That would be a terrible grand shame if they did."

Another pirate entered the room from the secret passageway to tie her hands. When he reached out to take the brooch clipped to her shawl, O'Grady stopped him.

Her face wrinkled into a dark scowl.

"Don't touch it, Ned," she warned. "Unless, you've a desire to be cursed. I saw with m' own eyes that hellion banshee leave it on the altar for her. Don't go touching it."

"You killed Bangford." Kathleen gasped. "But how can that be? The surgeon said he fell from the tower stairs."

"It was no accident, if that is what you're thinking. I pushed him," said the unrepentant pirate. "He threatened me! I who helped him find the treasure map. He said he'd expose us to the authorities if we didn't do as he wished. He didn't want you to know anything. He wanted you to think him to be a proper gentleman, but he was always one of us, a pirate."

Although Ned didn't touch it, he continued to eye the brooch. She noted the greedy calculation in his dark eyes. If the enchanted piece of jewelry wasn't cursed by the dreadful banshee, it would be worth a small fortune. By the way his hand kept hovering, it was evident he wanted to take it.

Someone else noticed his reaction.

"I said t' keep yer hands off!" Mrs. O'Grady growled, coldly aiming the sharp end of a light sword at his throat.

"Do what I say and step away from her. We've work to do. And I need that chit to help us retrieve the cargo. The last thing I want is some wrathful spirit to come curse us to pieces because you up and provoked it."

"But what about the others?" he asked, referring to the pirates who were distracting the militia. "Why can't they help us?"

"I don't trust them," the female leader said. "The only reason those mercenaries came to help was because I paid them plenty of blunt for their services. Aye, I wouldn't turn my back on any of them. They'd put a bullet straight through me if they could."

They forcibly led Kathleen down into the secret passageway. As they entered, a shiver of fear went through her. She knew that the minute they laid their

Beverly Adam

hands on the cargo, her life would come to a sudden end.

The cold and dank tunnel snaked gently downwards into the ground below the hall. The brute lit a torch with a rag he held aloft in one scabbed hand.

They passed along dripping stone walls. It was evident the tunnel had not been built overnight. She sensed that it had been constructed hundreds of years before Dovehill Hall, possibly by the Catholic monks.

The passageway consisted of a maze. In the dark she tried to get her bearings. She wanted to be certain to remember the way out, if she managed to escape. Off-shooting tunnels confused the direction they were traveling in. It would be easy to become lost in the dark.

As they rounded a corner, a skeleton's head leered down at her from a stone shelf. A black spider dropped down on a clear thread from its exposed teeth onto her shoulder.

She gave a frightened scream, shaking.

It fell harmlessly to the ground.

"Stop wailing," said Mrs. O'Grady sternly. "You'll be seeing plenty more of those where we're going—so ye best get used to it."

"The catacombs . . ." Kathleen whispered with sudden realization.

They were about to enter the common burial grounds located below the monastery. She had never before been inside them. Her husband had never permitted it. Now she knew why. And she had to face the terrible reality she might soon be joining the dead monks entombed there.

They slowed their pace. Sensing they were nearing the end, she looked for a sharp object with which to cut through the ropes. It would be the only way to escape. She was too far down in the ground for any cries of help to be heard.

On a low-lying shelf she noticed a skeleton. It

looked to be a warrior. He wore a round crown. It encircled his fleshless skull, a sign that he'd once been a local chieftain. In his crossed arms lay a small dagger. She noticed the empty spaces in this crown, which had once held precious gems. Grave robbers, no doubt, had removed them.

But the dagger, which was considered of no particular value, had been left in his hands. His other was empty. It probably had once held a long broad sword, evidence that he had once been a great warrior. A large leather shield lay on his chest. To be buried here, instead of on a battle ground, meant his life ended only when he was defeated by the Grim Reaper, death itself.

They stopped for a few minutes as the pirates consulted a map. She took the opportunity to step backwards. She pried the small weapon from the dead chieftain's hand, hiding her actions in the shadows.

Slowly—with clumsy skill, she began to slice away at the binding rope.

"Are you certain it's to the right?" she heard Ned ask.

"What are ye, moonstruck or something? I told you t' look for the markings. Why the devil are you using that worthless piece of parchment?" Mrs. O'Grady sneered. "Or don't you remember the last time we were down here? We were lost for over two hours. And that was because you trusted this useless bit of tree shavings."

The female pirate snatched the map from his hand and set it on fire. The parchment momentarily brightened the chamber. It flamed as it smoked and fell to the ground. For a moment the dagger cast a shadow on the wall behind her.

Frightened, Kathleen held her breath, waiting for her secret to be discovered, but her captors were too involved with their own private dispute to notice the weapon in her hands.

"Why did ye do that?" the shocked pirate asked. "What if we become lost? We have no way of knowing how to get out of here."

"Because," said Mrs. O'Grady, "you'll now be forced to obey me. Something you haven't been doing. Now get on with it and follow the markings like I told ye to."

The rope suddenly grew slack . . . Kathleen had managed to saw through the cords. She was free. Keeping her hands behind her, she knew she had to patiently choose her moment to try and escape.

Beau returned to the dining room. The doors were locked, as he expected. But as Kathleen did not let him in, he forced them open.

Entering the empty room, he noticed with alarm the opened passageway.

He called urgently to the armed militia to join him. He knew she wouldn't have gone down into the tunnels without him. She had to have been forced.

"Lady Langtry has been taken by the pirates," he said to the captain as way of explanation when he appeared. "We have to go after her."

He grabbed the lit candelabra from the dining table to use as a light. He had no idea where the tunnels might lead, what perils might lie ahead, but he was determined to find her at all cost.

He couldn't bear contemplating what might be happening to her, if she came to any harm. He felt an icy lump in his throat at the thought. He'd never forgive himself.

She'd become the center of his world. He could no longer imagine his life without her. He would save her. He had to.

*　*　*

Kathleen and the pirates arrived in front of a shallow

cave. A strange rotten-egg smell permeated the air around them. A heavily chained fence bordered the cave. Piled inside were barrels of black-market Portuguese port, French silk, and stacked boxes of antiquities—all illegal booty the pirates had stolen from both the living and the dead.

Next to it were small barrels of gunpowder. Seeing it, her heart pounded with excited hope. It was in that instant she knew how she was going to make her escape. And she had to time it perfectly or quite possibly lose her own life.

The pirates sacrilegiously sifted through the belongings of the dead. Carelessly, they tossed about the religious relics. It didn't matter to them that the priceless artifacts had once belonged to druid kings and holy monks.

They suddenly heard an eerie scream, echoing down through the tunnels.

A cool wind blew swiftly past them. Shivering with fear, they turned to see where the gust originated from.

The glowing figure of the female banshee quickly took shape before their startled eyes.

"What the devil—" sputtered Ned, as he was about to smash the gems off a cross.

The spirit opened wide its mouth. A piercing scream of rage emitted from the being. Her glowing hand pointed to the treasure. She screamed again, causing the torches' flames to quiver.

While Mrs. O'Grady and the pirate stood frozen by the banshee, Kathleen rushed over to the powder. The banshee was providing her with the distraction she needed. Pushing the ropes off, she removed her hands from behind her back.

Gently, she placed a powder keg on its side. She pushed it up the tunnel floor to where it began to turn a corner.

"What do ye think yer doing?" asked Ned, turning around, discovering that their captive had set herself free.

She grabbed the torch that hung above her head.

"I'm giving you to the banshee," she said with calm assurance, certain the spirit would take him to hell.

Uncorking the barrel, she kicked it towards him. It rolled, leaving a clear trail of dark powder. She tipped the flame. Igniting the explosive, it sparked with a deadly hiss. Dropping the torch, she ran.

*   *   *

Beau cautiously entered an off-shooting tunnel from the secret passageway. He could not see anything ahead, but pitch blackness. The moment his foot touched down, he heard an earth shattering explosion. The ear-bursting sound echoed through the tunnels. Bits of fragmented rocks fell around them.

For a moment he lost his footing. Frightened, he realized Kathleen might be down where the explosion originated. Holding the candelabra, he began to run as fast as he could, not knowing where the passageway would lead.

The militia tried to follow, but quickly lost him.

"Kathleen!" he yelled, panicking at the thought that she might somehow be hurt or trapped in the dark below. What if she was suffocating?

He had to find her! He berated himself for the one-hundredth time. How could he have been so foolish as to leave her unprotected? How easily he had let her fall into those villains' hands.

In his mind he pictured her face, imagining frightened eyes staring at him. His heart twisted painfully. He should never have left her alone. He had to rescue her, even if it meant tearing apart the tunnels stone by stone.

* * *

Breathless, not looking where she was going, Kathleen ran straight into a solid form. It was a man. She looked up into her beloved's face.

"Beau . . ." She breathed, her heart thudding with relief.

"Thank heavens," he said.

He clasped her to him, tightly holding onto her as if he feared she would suddenly disappear. She hugged him. She had never felt anything as good as his arms around her. "You're alive," he said.

"I managed to escape," she explained. "I cut the ropes they used to bind me using a small dagger. And then I set off an explosion with gunpowder."

"You did that . . ." he said with admiration in his voice, but then added as an afterthought, "but you might have been killed, possibly caught up in the blast and blown to bits!"

Touching her talisman, she said, "I had no choice. It was that or let myself be led to the slaughter, like a willing pig. And I swore to God I would not do that. I took my chance." She gave a shaky laugh. "My guardian saints were with me. I lit the gunpowder and introduced those two villains to Beelzebub himself."

"Yes." He nodded proudly, realizing how strong she truly was. "You freed yourself and defeated them . . . the fools . . . they didn't know they were dealing with the bravest woman in Ireland."

"I thought . . ." She swallowed, unable to finish the thought. It was too painful. She'd thought she would never be with him again.

"You thought what, dear heart?" he asked gently, smoothing her hair back from her face with a shaking hand.

She shook her head. Tears sprang in her eyes as she buried her face into his shoulder.

When she was a captive, she'd been afraid. She thought she was going to die. She'd wanted to tell him how grateful she was for all the help and support he'd given her. He had opened her heart again.

"Come, let's leave this place," he said, putting his arms around her shoulders. He noticed she'd begun to shake from the cold. Concerned with her health, he quickly led her back out through the tunnels.

Halfway up, they encountered the militia, with the local captain of the guard leading them.

"Thank heavens, you're alive. We thought we'd lost you, Lady Langtry," the captain said, visibly relieved at the sight of the young woman walking beside the tall magistrate.

"My men discovered a tunnel blown asunder. All that remains is a pile of rubble. We feared the worst had happened to you."

"No, I am still quite alive," she said with a small smile. But curiosity caused her to ask, "Did you come across anyone else?"

He shook his head.

"Other than the dead saints who lie beneath," he said, "we met no one. It would appear that if anyone had been breathing down there, they are no longer. It is what it has been for quite some time, a burial ground for the dead."

"And I will make certain it remains so," she said.

Shakily, she thought of the people she'd killed. Although they'd been murderous villains, hell bent on destroying her, it troubled her conscience.

Thinking of the banshee spirit who'd guided her, she resolved never again to disturb the dead. She did not want the ancient tombs to be opened and exposed to the greed of men. She would make certain of that as the mistress of Dovehill Hall.

Chapter 13

The mercenary pirates, who'd remained above ground, were caught and put into the militia's armed custody and carted off to face a sentencing tribunal in Dublin, while the Countess Deuville and her son, Henry, were exiled to one of his majesty's penal colonies.

The local guarda and the militia were both given credit for capturing the dangerous villains, generating a rare but important feeling of unified accomplishment between the Irish and the English.

As for the newly resurrected Captain Fitzpatrick, it was learned that he had had quite an adventure before reaching Ireland again. As reported, The Blue Star had indeed run into a gale as it rounded the cape of South Africa's horn. The crew took to the longboats as the ship hit sharp reefs off the African coast, rowing in the direction of the nearby shore. That was the last time he saw his crew alive. James had been the last man to jump ship, miraculously making it to shore by the use of his own limbs and the ship's floating wreckage.

"What became of my men, I do not know," he said grimly. "I fear a fierce warrior tribe may have captured and killed them. I was lost in the jungles for two years, at one point succumbing to malaria, living for a time with some Jesuit priests. When at last I reached civilization, I had to earn my passage back home. I would have returned two weeks ago if it hadn't been for those interfering pirates. They captured the vessel I was on and decided to hold me for ransom when they learned that my wife's niece was none other than the Earl of Drennan's wealthy bride. They were about to contact you for the money, but my beloved wife rescued me before they had a chance."

"You're back home now, James," said Agnes consolingly, holding tightly his arm. "And we will never again be parted."

"Aye that's for sure, love," he replied fondly. Patting her hand, he silently vowed never again to set foot on a ship. He envisioned a future of spending his twilight years in a small cottage with his beloved wife, near the sea, looking, but never sailing it.

Kathleen decided to host a celebratory ball to honor the local villagers and the militia. It also allowed her to make amends for her late husband's questionable involvement with the illegal smuggling.

She'd spent the past few weeks with the household staff preparing for the festivities. As mistress of the hall, she'd begun to put her personal mark upon the estate. Subtle changes had been made to the grounds surrounding the square building. Vines and flowering bushes had been planted, softening the harsh look of the Gothic exterior.

Now when she strolled around the hall, she no longer stiffened with discomfort. It was truly becoming her home. A place she felt comfortable and happy in, where she might one day raise a family.

"What do you want me to do with this, my lady?" asked a liveried footman, carrying one of her late husband's large marble elephants.

He held it up for her inspection.

The white elephant was gilded purple, pink, and gold. She remembered it being placed next to her husband's bishop's chair, the memory of which made her inwardly cringe.

It was gaudy, she quickly decided. She would have had it tossed into the rubbish heap, if it weren't for the fact that it was gilded in real gold. She wrinkled her nose. What to do with it? Should she try and sell it?

She said with open dislike, "Place it by the ballroom

door. And the first person who comments on how lovely and tasteful it is, hand it to them to carry back home—I have no further use for it."

Little by little she'd been emptying the hall of the ornate bric-a-brac her late husband had collected. She had them auctioned off and the money donated to various charitable organizations. Her generous philanthropy was to be remembered by many. It helped erase the black mark her dead husband's illegal activities had left.

And it served another purpose. It kept the interfering British government at bay. Under normal circumstances they would have swooped in and confiscated Dovehill Hall, heartlessly casting her out onto the dirt road. They could have easily used Bangford's black-market activities as an excuse to claim the hall and its adjoining estates for their own. But they didn't.

Both Beau and the British militia's captain spoke out on her behalf. They recounted to the authorities how she had valiantly fought the pirates and by doing so, she had demonstrated her unquestionable loyalty to the crown.

Convinced of her innocence, those in power left her in peace. They permitted her to continue running Dovehill Hall's lucrative estates for the next generation to enjoy and for the British government to tax.

"Look what her ladyship gave me," she overheard an elderly sheepherder exclaim.

He tottered over to her with a big smile on his wrinkled face, proudly carrying the gaudy white elephant in his arms. A young man, his grandson, stood at his elbow to steady his grandfather, lest the tottering elder should suddenly lose his precarious balance.

"Many thanks to you, ma'am, for this fine elephant." He pulled on his thinned forelock in respect. "I shall treasure this for the remainder of m' living days," the sheepherder said. "I always did like exotic animals. And this one will look right grand over m' hearth."

"It is my pleasure, sir, to give it to you. I hope you enjoy it as much as my late husband did," she replied, thinking about the other exotic objects she wanted to rid herself of.

There must be at least a half dozen or more items I can give away, she decided, pleased that her plan had worked so well and had made someone else happy. But before she had an opportunity to find more, the orchestra struck up a regal tune—someone important had arrived.

It was the Earl of Drennan and his lovely new bride, Lady Beatrice, with her father and aunt, Lord Patrick O' Brien, and Lady Agnes and Captain Fitzpatrick. Their entrance caused quite a stir. They were the highest ranking landowners and nobility in the vicinity. To have them condescend to attend the ball was indeed a tribute to the hostess of Dovehill Hall. It was an official stamp of approval from the ruling aristocratic class. Her late husband's questionable activities were to be forgiven and forgotten.

She quickly walked over and gave a low curtsy of welcome. Beau, acting as her guardian and co-host, joined her. "How wonderful of you to come," she said, warmly embracing Lady Beatrice, the lady she had once helped rescue.

"The honor is all ours," replied the dark-haired lady, standing next to her husband, the Earl of Drennan, her aunt and the newly freed Captain Fitzpatrick.

"We would not dream of missing the celebration of the capture of those pirates who caused you and my uncle so much trouble. I am certain the entire village rejoices that your ladyship did not come to any harm."

Kathleen could not help but notice that Lady Beatrice wore an evening gown with a train for the special occasion. Her attire was as much a complement to the importance of the festivity as was her presence.

The gown was made of fine black silk edged in matching lace. Her ladyship's jewelry, family heirlooms that had been passed from one generation to the next, sparkled at her throat and dangled fetchingly from her ears. Her long black hair was swept up in the Grecian style and strands of pearls were entwined in her hair.

There was not a single person in the room who was not a little awed. Lady Langtry's esteemed guests were the epitome of what Irish aristocracy ought to aspire to be. They were known to be strong of character, hard-working, and forward thinking. There wasn't a man or woman in the room who didn't want to be connected to them.

"Indeed, I was most fortunate to be aided and protected by our local guarda and the British militia. I thank you for your kind wishes for my well-being," she replied. "But please do us the honor of joining in the dance, in celebration. It would be a great pleasure for our guests if you were to do so."

"It would be our delight," replied the earl on his wife's behalf, smiling, giving his official seal of approval. He turned towards his friend Beau and greeted him warmly.

Holding out his gloved hand for his wife to take, they decorously prepared to dance, as the orchestra struck up music for a stately quadrille.

Couples stood in a square, a pair located at each of the corners. The word for the dance originated from this formation, meaning four or quad. In the early nineteenth century, elements from this dance would develop into the waltz. Both dances had the rhythmic beat of 2/4 time.

All stood back and watched. It was a memorable event for the entire village. And the reputation of Dovehill Hall was completely repaired. No one wished ill of the brave, young widow who had escaped and helped capture the most dangerous pirates in Ireland.

"Aye, for sure now," many said. "'Twas surely no wonder that Lord Bangford died from the banshee's curse. He was an evil man and deserved it. But now may his pretty, young widow live in peace. May she be blessed with a good man, like her guardian, Master Powers, for a husband. The solicitor has already done well by taking good care of both her ladyship and Dovehill Hall. Aye, the sweet mistress deserves to be treated with respect. She should have a happy life after having faced down those thieving pirates."

It was with great pride the tenants and those in service at Dovehill Hall watched their lady dance with the solicitor. Many began speculating if wedding banns might soon be posted. It wouldn't surprise them if they did. The romantic way the couple gazed at each other proclaimed their tender feelings.

*　*　*

After their guests had left, Beau and Kathleen strolled quietly by the lake. The moon shone clearly upon the water as the two walked, hand-in-hand, along the edge. Tim ran down the lawn in front of them.

Kathleen unwittingly shuddered. She fingered the enchanted brooch, remembering she had stood at this very spot and observed the banshee wailing, the night her husband had died and she was freed from his tyrannical control.

"Are you cold?" Beau asked, placing an arm around her.

"No, I'm fine . . . I was remembering the night Bangford died."

She drew closer. The feel of his arms around her was comforting. He'd shared in the dangers she'd faced.

Courageously, he'd protected her, never giving a thought to his own safety. He had put her first.

Looking out at the lake, she contemplated her life. Orphaned at a young age and then sold by her greedy uncle, she'd been the child bride of a controlling lord. She'd been made a prisoner in her own home, which was ruled over by a dangerous woman, the housekeeper, a female pirate smuggler, but whereas before she had been alone, dominated, and made to feel small, she was no longer. Beau now stood solidly beside her.

He'd helped her from the minute she'd buried her husband up to this moment. Because of him, she was able to live the life she'd always dreamed. She was empowered. She'd faced down death and was no longer afraid that any man would again completely control her life.

She looked up at his profile and tried to picture her life without him. She could not. He'd become too important.

"Beau," she said looking up into his eyes. "I have made an important decision and I need you, as my guardian, to agree to it."

"And what would that be?"

"A special love charm was cast upon me," she said, touching her brooch lightly. "And I have no desire to be cured of it. Indeed, I would like very much for it to continue to enchant me. If you're agreeable . . . and in love with me . . . I would like you to ask me to be your wife."

He blinked then gave a shout of laughter.

He turned to her, and gently cupped her face; a tender smile lit his.

"Vixen," he said, "You've become quite your own woman."

"Yes," she smiled, "but you have become the other half my heart has been longing for. I think it will break if you do not become completely mine."

"Well, we mustn't have that, now must we?" He smiled and went down on one knee.

He took her hand and gallantly asked the question she most longed to hear, "Kathleen, you are the woman I have been looking for all of my life. You're strong, brave, and yes, beautiful, as well as amazingly resourceful . . . all qualities which I greatly admire. You have made me feel a jumble of emotions that I have never felt before, from terrifying fear to sweet, heady desire. Darling, I cannot imagine my life continuing without you in it. I am in love with you. Please, will you marry me and make me the happiest of men?"

She laughed with delight, nodded her head, and said, "Yes—Yes, I will."

He stood and took her into his arms. They shared a kiss that warmed her heart and changed her life. Never again was she to be alone. Their lives were to be filled with the challenging adventure of raising a family, running an estate, and being completely enchanted by each other.

About the Author

Engaging, romantic frolics, with a touch of magic, are how author, Beverly Adam, describes her Regency Romance series: *Gentlemen of Honor*. The redheaded writer currently resides in California where she revisits history on a regular basis as a romance novelist and biographer.

www.ingramcontent.com/pod-product-compliance
Lightning Source LLC
Chambersburg PA
CBHW070749180626
46818CB00007B/3052